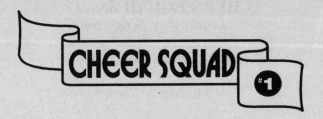

CRAZY FOR CARTWHEELS

Shannon

Other Avon Camelot Books in the
CHEER SQUAD *Series by*
Linda Joy Singleton

SPIRIT SONG

Coming Soon

STAND UP AND CHEER!

LINDA JOY SINGLETON has written nearly twenty young adult and middle grade novels, including the *My Sister, The Ghost* series. While she never was a cheerleader, as a teenager she performed with a round dance group called the Silhouettes. In her twenties, she and her husband, David, square danced professionally with the Rainbow Stars. And as part of her research into cheerleading, she has enrolled in a ballet class.

She lives near Sacramento on three country acres with her husband and two kids, Melissa and Andy. They have lots of animals: dogs, cats, ducks, chickens, goats, and two horses.

CHEER SQUAD #1

CRAZY FOR CARTWHEELS

LINDA JOY SINGLETON

AN AVON CAMELOT BOOK

CHEER SQUAD #1: CRAZY FOR CARTWHEELS is an original publication of Avon Books. This work has never before appeared in book form.

AVON BOOKS
A division of
The Hearst Corporation
1350 Avenue of the Americas
New York, New York 10019

Copyright © 1996 by Linda Joy Singleton
Excerpt from *Cheer Squad #2: Spirit Song* copyright © 1996 by Linda Joy Singleton
Published by arrangement with the author
Library of Congress Catalog Card Number: 96-96086
ISBN: 0-380-78438-6
RL: 4.9

First Avon Camelot Printing: September 1996

CAMELOT TRADEMARK REG. U.S. PAT. OFF. AND IN OTHER COUNTRIES, MARCA REGISTRADA, HECHO EN U.S.A.

Printed in the U.S.A.

OPM   10 9 8 7 6 5 4 3 2

With special thanks to my high school friend, Dori Smithee. And her daughter, Jennifer Smithee, of the Tokay Cheerleaders.

● ● ● ● ● ● ● ● ● ● ●

One

Green and gold pompons were poised at my sides, ready to take flight and swirl like colorful kaleidoscopes. My whole body tensed; eager, nervous, and so excited I could barely breathe. Lights glowed and flashed everywhere: bright overhead lights, the cameras of proud parents, and even TV cameras. This was the big one, the most important cheerleading event of all—the National Cheerleading Competition. And I was part of it. Me! Ordinary Wendi Holcroft from Kalaroosa County!

There was a hush in the auditorium. Expectations mounted. I glanced at my teammates. Great friends, hard workers, dream sharers. We'd come a long way, and now we were ready to show the world that together we could achieve anything. Maybe even first place. . . .

The music started, and low applause rose until it echoed off the walls. I lifted my pompons and awaited my cue, ready to jump, toe touch, and cartwheel into stardom.

Cheerleaders on your marks, get set, and—

"Wendi! Why are you hugging your pillow?" came a loud shout that burst into Wendi's head like an explosion. "Save the hugs for your first boyfriend—or else you'll squeeze the stuffing right out of your pillow."

Wendi recognized her older sister Valerie's amused voice, and reality set in. She wasn't at the nationals. She wasn't even cheerleading. She was in her own bed.

"Huh?" Wendi mumbled, blinking up at her sister. As usual, Valerie's red-gold hair fell around her shoulders in soft, shiny waves. Wendi thought she looked like a model from a fashion magazine. "I-I guess I was dreaming. Is it time to get up already?"

"You bet it is," Valerie said with a wide grin. It was the same grin that Wendi often admired when she flipped through Valerie's cheerleading scrapbook. Now that Valerie was in college, though, she'd decided to give up cheers and back flips for textbooks and a major in child psychology.

"So what were you dreaming about?" Valerie sat on the edge of the bed. "Some cute guy, right?"

"Wrong," Wendi said, feeling her cheeks heat up.

"You're blushing!" Valerie exclaimed. "He must be really cute. What's his name?"

"There's no guy. Honestly. I was dreaming

about cheerleading. Today the tryout results will be posted. Tabby and I can't wait to find out if we made the squad."

"You guys can't miss. You've been practicing all summer. You two are fantastic!" Valerie said in her best rah-rah voice. After all, she'd been a cheerleader in junior high and high school. She'd won lots of awards, and her squad even took first place in the varsity division at the nationals.

All Wendi's life, she'd admired her older sister's many accomplishments: gymnastics, ballet, cheerleading, and straight A's. In Wendi's eyes, Valerie was *perfect*. And Wendi wanted to be perfect, too. She just *had* to become a cheerleader.

"I really hope we make it," Wendi said, pushing back her tangled auburn hair. She remembered the tryout clinic last month and felt uneasy. She and her best friend, Tabby, (her real name was Tabitha) had done their best. Their kicks had been high, their cheers enthusiastic, and Wendi had done an aerial that practically defied gravity. But had their best been good enough? It hadn't in sixth grade, when everything was a popularity event. And Wendi and Tabby were only medium popular.

In sixth grade, girls like Darlene Dittman and LaShaun Penner had been voted in as cheerleaders. Darlene had been taking jazz dance classes for years and had some great moves. But she was a know-it-all who acted really bossy. And LaShaun was an okay gymnast, but her rhythm was off. Her kicks were always a beat behind. Still, Darlene and LaShaun were megapopular. And since popularity meant votes, Darlene and her friends had made the squad, but Wendi and Tabby hadn't.

Of course, that was sixth grade, Wendi thought. *Elementary school. In junior high, talent and hard work are more important than how many friends you have. And Tabby and I really worked hard all summer, studying video tapes of Valerie's national competitions. I used my computer to create some awesome routines. And Tabby combined fancy ballet moves with gymnastic stunts. And we both practiced, practiced, practiced!*

Wendi was starting to feel confident about making the squad until she glanced into her bedroom mirror, saw a flash of silver, and remembered the awful thing that had happened right before tryouts. Her family dentist had said her teeth were slightly crooked, and she needed to wear braces for six months.

It's impossible to keep your teeth hidden while cheerleading, which had made trying out really hard. And the worst part was when she had overheard Darlene call her "Metal Mouth." Talk about embarrassed! Still, Wendi had held her head high, focused on her performance, and cheered her heart out.

Her routine had felt better than ever. And Tabby had done great, too—and today they would find out the tryout results.

Will we be popularity rejects? Wendi wondered. *Or will we become Castle Hill cheerleaders?*

When Wendi stepped off the school bus later that morning, the second Monday of junior high,

Tabby rushed out to meet her. Tabby's light-brown hair was twisted into a French braid, and she wore her lucky tiger-striped T-shirt.

"Wendi!" Tabby cried, falling in step with her best friend. "I've been going crazy waiting for you. Are you as nervous as I am?"

"Worse," Wendi admitted, loosening her backpack straps so they didn't dig into her shoulders. "Are the results posted?"

"Yes." Tabby's green eyes grew somber as she nodded. "But I haven't had the courage to look yet. After all our practicing, I'll be devastated if we didn't make it."

"Me, too," Wendi said.

"I'm sure you'll make the squad," Tabby said. "Your aerial was awesome!"

"But I might have lost points for my smile." Wendi covered her mouth with her hand, wishing she could rip off her silver braces.

"I hardly notice your braces. But I'm so short, my kicks might not have been high enough," Tabby fretted. "And I really want to be involved in sports this year. It would be cool to cheer for football. Even Adam would be impressed."

Wendi nodded, knowing that Tabby was more interested in impressing her father, who worked as a college football coach, than her ninth-grade brother, Adam. Her parents were divorced, so Tabby only saw her father on occasional weekends and holidays. He had never attended any of Tabby's dance recitals, although he regularly showed up for Adam's football games.

As Wendi and Tabby passed the office, they

saw a group of girls buzzing around the library, where there was a large bulletin board. Wendi spotted Darlene's sleek crown of white-blond hair. Even from a distance, Wendi could tell that Darlene was elated. The slender blond girl jumped up and down, smiling at nearby girls. Wendi's heart sank. Darlene had definitely made the squad.

But what about me? Wendi wondered, torn between worry, fear, and hope. *And what about Tabby?*

Suddenly, Wendy was terrified to read the list. She shared a nervous look with Tabby. A school warning bell rang, but they ignored it.

Now was the moment of truth.

Only a few girls still mulled around the list. Most had gone on to their classes, Wendi guessed, including Darlene—thank goodness.

"You check first," Tabby whispered, clinging to Wendi's arm.

"All right."

Wendi could hardly hear her own voice over her pounding heart. The list loomed ahead. How strange that a simple piece of white paper could control her junior high destiny . . . maybe the entire course of her future.

Since eighth grade cheerleaders had been chosen last spring, only seventh graders were on the list: six regular spots and two alternates.

Right away Wendi saw Darlene's name. And no wonder, since Darlene's father was listed as the new squad coach. Wendi had heard that Coach Emburg had moved away unexpectedly a few weeks ago, but she hadn't realized Darlene's father had taken over the job. What did the owner of a plumbing company know about cheerleading?

Wendi read through the rest of the names. LaShaun Penner, Jennifer Huong, Penny Nicholas, Angela Brazelli, Kayla Tracey, Kimberly Aldrich . . .

Beside her, Wendi heard Tabby gasp. Wendi thought she may have gasped, too, but she was too stunned to notice. The paper read like a Who's Who of Darlene's circle of friends, as if Darlene had personally picked which girls she wanted as seventh grade cheerleaders. Wendi and Tabby's names were *not* listed.

Wendi blinked back tears. All her hard work and practice had counted for nothing.

Once again, she was a popularity reject.

Two

"It's just not fair!" Tabby exclaimed as they walked into the cafeteria a few hours later. "I can't stop thinking about the list. It's so unfair."

A lump rose in Wendi's throat, and she nodded. She knew exactly how Tabby felt.

As they walked to a table in the back, Wendi tried to ignore the smiling faces of the seventh grade cheerleaders sitting at a front table. Darlene reigned as queen. And Wendi and Tabby were locked out of the castle gates.

"Maybe we should complain to the principal," Tabby suggested, stabbing a straw through the top of her milk carton. Wendi had never seen her friend so angry. Tabby was usually easygoing. But then, Wendi felt angry, too.

"Why bother?" Wendi asked, spreading her palms in a defeated gesture. She took a tuna fish sandwich out of her sack lunch. "If Coach Emburg hadn't moved away, I'm positive we would have made the squad. But with Darlene's father as coach, we never had a real chance."

"I bet Mr. Dittman never even looked at the tryout results—he probably just let his precious Darlene pick and choose," Tabby said angrily.

Wendi scowled. "Let's just forget cheerleading. You can go back to dance class, and I'll focus on gymnastics. On the tumbling mat, my back flips count more than a perfect smile."

"There's nothing wrong with your smile," Tabby said. "You're just oversensitive about your braces because of Darlene's nasty remarks. I think your braces are kind of pretty. Like jewelry for your teeth."

"Nice try. But I know my smile looks gross," Wendi said, then took a bite of her sandwich. A piece of tuna got stuck on her top brace and she pushed it away with her tongue.

Wendi looked up as a girl with wild honey-blond hair came toward them. She wore really dramatic clothes: a bright multicolored vest over a mint-green shirt, a metallic purple skirt, and bobbing fish-shaped earrings. Wendi thought she looked familiar.

"You're Wendi and Tabitha, aren't you?" the blond girl asked in an excited rush.

"Everyone calls me Tabby."

"Yeah, I'm Wendi. Do I know you? Wait . . . now I remember. You were at the cheerleading tryouts last month! I remember being impressed with your booming voice."

"I'm a loudmouth and proud of it!" She laughed and sat across from them. "I'm Krystal Carvell.

And I'll never forget that knock-'em-dead aerial you did."

Tabby flashed Wendi a proud smile. "Wendi's been practicing cheers since she could walk. She got me interested in cheerleading."

"You were both super! Which is why I freaked when I didn't see your names on the list," Krystal said, frowning. "My best friend, Anna, and I didn't make it either, and I know we were good, too. The new coach doesn't know anything about real talent."

"He's Darlene's father," Wendi pointed out.

"You're kidding!" Krystal's blue eyes bulged. "Well, that explains everything. Darlene got really mad at me during tryouts when I said her hand motions were too jerky. I was trying to be helpful, but she blew up."

"Darlene thinks she knows everything," Tabby said.

"Well, she's wrong," Krystal declared. "Her hand motions *are* jerky. I could have helped her if she'd listened. I've been studying all kinds of dance since I was little, when my parents used to take my on their road trips."

"Road trips?" Wendi asked, raising her brows.

"Yeah." Krystal grinned. "My mom works for a company that manages music groups. Their hottest talent right now is Badd Wrap. So you can see, performing is in my blood. But it's kind of hard for a twelve-year-old to get a gig, so I figured I'd perform as a cheerleader first. But I guess I blew it when I ticked Darlene off."

"Don't let Darlene get to you," Wendi said sympathetically.

"The tryout clinic was a waste of time," Tabby griped. "Darlene's father wasn't even there. And now Darlene has turned a team sport into a popularity contest."

"And we lost the contest," Krystal said with a sad sigh.

"Hey, Krystal," a petite black-haired girl called out, waving a paper as she came over. "Wait till you hear the news!"

Krystal looked up, grinned, then quickly introduced her friend as Anna Hererra. Anna's smile was huge, and her black eyes sparkled with excitement. Wendi remembered watching her audition and thinking Anna was the happiest girl she'd ever seen.

"What's up, Anna?" Krystal asked, making room for her friend at the table.

"Well, you know my brother Esteban is really into basketball," Anna began, speaking fast and in a soft, rhythmic voice.

"Yeah." Krystal blushed a bit. "He's the best player on the team. So, what?"

"Well, I just ran into him and he told me that the Castle Hill Cheerleaders have decided to cut the basketball team from their cheering schedule. They claim they'll be *too* busy."

"Busy doing what?" Wendi asked. "Football season is over by the time basketball season starts. I think Darlene just doesn't want to cheer for a team that lost every game last year."

"You're probably right. Which is great for us,"

Anna said excitedly. She thrust a paper toward Krystal. "Look what my brother gave me! It's like a miracle. Something to be really glad about!"

Curious, Wendi leaned forward. It was a printed form and the top words snared her interest: NEW CHEERLEADING SQUAD. It went on to announce that the basketball team wanted to start their own cheerleading squad. It would be a "no cut" squad, which meant that anyone who signed up made the squad. It was being sponsored by the boys' basketball coach, Mr. Kendall. All interested seventh and eighth graders were invited to join.

"Wow!" Wendi murmured, feeling excited and hopeful all over again. Anna was right. This was a miracle—a second chance to make their cheerleading dreams come true.

And Wendi couldn't wait to sign up.

● ● ● ● ● ● ● ● ● ●

Three

All Wendi could think about as she walked home from school that day was the new cheer squad. Tabby was at her weekly meeting for gifted kids, so Wendi was alone with just her daydreams.

It would be torture waiting four days to begin her career as a cheerleader—not till Friday, after school. She and Tabby had already signed up. In fact, Wendi's name had been the first on the list, followed by Tabby, Krystal, and Anna. The four were the only names so far—a great start! And since this was a "no cut" squad, no one would be excluded this time. They were so eager to get started cheering together that they were all going to practice tonight at Wendi's house.

It was like a fairy godmother had waved a magic wand and answered Wendi's heartfelt wishes with this thrilling opportunity! And the best part was that bossy Queen Darlene wouldn't be running their squad. That meant Wendi's own leadership skills could shine and she *might* have a chance to fulfill another one of her dreams: being squad captain.

Pausing at a corner, she grew serious as she thought this over. Tabby would vote for her. Maybe even Krystal and Anna. And Wendi would vote for herself. But if the team had ten or twelve members, four votes might not be enough. Besides, Krystal had a dynamic and outgoing personality. What if she decided to go out for team captain, too? Would the others think Krystal had more leadership qualities?

I'm getting way ahead of things, Wendi realized, smiling at herself. *We haven't even had one meeting of our new squad. After we know how many girls sign up, then I can worry about being captain.*

When Wendi reached her L-shaped brick house, she was bursting to talk to someone.

"Valerie, listen up!" she exclaimed to her older sister as she swept into the living room. "You won't believe what happened!"

Valerie put down a textbook and looked up with a smile. "By that grin on your face, I guess I'm talking to the newest member of the Castle Hill Cheerleaders."

"*Wrong!*" Wendi shook her head, causing her ponytail to brush her cheek. "Guess again."

"Huh?" Valerie raised her brows. "Didn't you make the squad?"

"Not exactly." Wendi paused and then launched into the whole story: Queen Darlene, the Who's Who list of football cheerleaders, and the new no-cut basketball cheerleading squad. When Wendi was done, she let out an exhausted breath, then sank on the couch next to her sister.

"A new squad at Castle Hill Junior High?" Valerie's eyes widened. "You're kidding me! Things have sure changed."

"You're the one who's always saying cheerleading is a constantly changing sport," Wendi pointed out.

"Changing, growing, and finally gaining athletic respect." Valerie squeezed her sister's hand. "Scholarships, camps, competitions—and someday the Olympics. Maybe in a few years I'll be cheering *you* on in some faraway country as an official slips a gold medal around your neck."

"Wouldn't that be great? But first I have to get on a squad. And a new squad will need lots of organizing. I don't know what Coach Kendall has planned, but we'll need uniforms, original routines, and a squad captain." Wendi chewed her lower lip and tried to calm the butterflies swarming in her stomach. "Which means megawork. Tabby and two new friends are coming over soon. I thought we'd practice some four-person routines, and I could really use your help. Will you coach us?"

"I'd love to, but I've got to cram for a psych quiz." Valerie pointed to a stack of books on an end table. "I'll be up past midnight studying."

Wendi tried to hide her disappointment. She'd really hoped Valerie could teach them a fantastic routine. Also, Wendi had secretly wanted to show off her talented, gorgeous sister to Krystal and Anna.

For the next few hours, Wendi was busy. Her parents got home from work, and Wendi helped her father make spaghetti for dinner. After dinner, Wendi accessed the computer's encyclopedia and printed out information on basketball as well as some cheerleading routine ideas.

By six-thirty, Wendi was poised by the huge window in her living room, waiting for her friends to show up. Tabby lived nearby in the Quail Oaks Apartments complex, so she was the first to arrive.

When Wendi opened the door, Tabby stood there holding a set of red-and-white pompons that once belonged to Valerie. Tabby waved the poms and bounced into the room. "Give me a S-Q-U-A-D . . . give me a new basketball squad!" she chanted.

"You've definitely got the S-P-I-R-I-T," Wendi teased as she shut the door.

"So where are the others?" Tabby looked around. "Are Krystal and Anna here yet?"

"They'll be here soon. Anna said her aunt was driving them over."

"Then I have time to give my favorite male a big kiss," Tabby said with a grin. "Where is Rufus?"

"Probably on top of the refrigerator. You know how he loves heights," Wendi said, following her friend into the kitchen. And sure enough, curled up on top of the fridge was a large orange-striped cat with a smug look around his whiskers. He let out a gravelly meow when he saw Tabby. She loved animals, especially cats, but unfortunately pets weren't allowed in her apartment.

While Tabby cuddled the cat, Wendi went back to the living room to wait for the others. She heard a loud rumbling sound outside and peered out the window.

"What in the world is *that?*" she muttered, staring at the strange contraption that was pulling up in front of her house. It was an old car with bright silver hubcaps; large, shiny black doors; and a weird rounded hood decorated with a golden bird.

The car door opened, and Krystal, Anna, and an elegant, slender woman with upswept raven hair stepped out onto the sidewalk. The woman carried herself like royalty: straight back, head high, and she glided rather than walked.

"This is my Aunt Carlotta—Mrs. Castle," Anna said, flashing her usual cheery smile.

"Glad to meet you, girls," the older woman said.

"My aunt runs a dance studio downtown," Anna told the other girls.

"You're all welcome to come by any time," Mrs. Castle said. She told Anna she would return for her and Krystal in a few hours. Then she climbed in the car, revved it up loudly, and roared away.

"Let's go in the backyard to practice," Wendi said, leading her friends through a side gate.

"Right behind you," Tabby said.

"We can start with warm-up exercises," Wendi

suggested. "Then I'll show you the info on basketball and cheer moves I printed out on my computer."

"Sounds great!" Anna said, shutting the gate behind her.

"I hope you included some stunts," Krystal said, slipping off a baggy tie-dyed shirt, revealing a stretchy two-piece shorts and top set. Her wild mane of blond hair was tamed with a gold scrunchie. And she had brought a set of gold pompons with her. "I'm a good base if someone else wants to be a flyer."

Anna waved her hand. "I can be a flyer. Or maybe Tabby should, since she's the smallest."

Tabby grimaced, and Wendi knew her friend was embarrassed about being petite. On her first day of junior high, several kids had teased Tabby about looking like an elementary school kid. So Wendi wasn't surprised when Tabby shook her head and told Anna to go ahead and be a flyer.

"Not that we can do many stunts with just four cheerleaders," Tabby added as she warmed up with toe touches.

"There's plenty we can do," Wendi insisted in her best future-team-captain voice. "I thought we'd start out with a kick line, axle into splits, jumps, and then bring it all together with some funky moves."

For the next hour, the girls practiced gymnastic and dance steps and worked on cheers. Since Anna was the only one without pompons, Wendi loaned her an old white set of Valerie's.

During a break, Wendi thought about everyone's strengths and weaknesses. Krystal had sharp, dynamic moves—but her kicks didn't synchronize with the others. It was clear Krystal loved being the center of attention—maybe too much. And Tabby was strong on dance steps, weak on tumbling moves. Wendi decided to help coach Tabby on back flips. Anna had all the steps down, but she seemed a bit unsure of herself, like she was holding back. *Anna needs a boost of confidence,* Wendi thought. *I'll try to give her some pep talks.*

And finally, Wendi came to herself; strong on gymnastics but weak on presentation—when she yelled cheers, she kept thinking about her "metal mouth" smile. She wanted to put a horrible curse on her dentist, but instead she vowed to smile wider and cheer louder.

At eight o'clock, Wendi's mother told the girls that Anna's aunt had called to say she was on her way over.

"This has been a great practice!" Krystal said, slipping back on her tie-dyed shirt and picking up her pompons.

"Ditto, here!" Anna tightened her ponytail and smiled. "Wendi, thanks for inviting us. I'm so glad we met you and Tabby. Not making football cheerleader could end up being our lucky break."

"Lucky my foot!" Krystal said, playfully swatting Anna with a pompon. "Sometimes Anna is so cheerful, I want to scream. I'll bet she could find something to be glad about over pop quizzes, summer school, and poison oak. Maybe even Darlene Dittman!"

"I think we're all glad we aren't on the same squad as Darlene," Anna said teasingly.

Everyone laughed. To Wendi, the four of them already felt like a team. Practicing with Tabby had always been fun, and with Krystal and Anna, it was doubly fun.

There was a loud *ahooga* blast of a car horn.

"That's Aunt Carlotta," Anna said. "Come on, Krystal."

"Want to meet again tomorrow?" Wendi asked.

"Y-E-S!" Krystal chanted, waving her poms.

Anna and Tabby nodded, giggling. They all agreed to meet at six-thirty the following night and then once again on Thursday—the evening before the big event: *the first new squad meeting*.

Wendi went to sleep that night dreaming about pirouettes, toe touches, and back flips. When she had her favorite dream about competing at the nationals, she felt happier than ever because now she was one step closer to achieving her cheering goals.

When she awoke Tuesday morning, she felt hopeful and happy—which lasted until she reached school.

That's when Krystal rushed up with an I've-got-bad-news look on her face. Wendi's cheerful attitude immediately disappeared. She had a terrible feeling that after she heard Krystal's bad news, there would no longer be *anything* to be glad about.

Four

Even upset, Krystal looked dazzling. Today she wore hot-pink overalls, a shiny white blouse, hoop earrings, and a neon-mauve scrunchie around her ponytail. She frowned at Wendi and announced ominously, "We have a problem."

"We do?" Wendi twisted a metal chain around her bicycle spokes, fastened her lock, and turned to look up at Krystal.

"Do we ever!" Krystal said, gesturing dramatically with her hands. "A tragedy! A crisis! Major problem!"

"And for once Krystal's not exaggerating," Anna said, coming up to stand beside Krystal. Anna's thick black hair was puffed up and pulled back in a gold butterfly clip, and she wore stonewashed jeans and a baggy strawberry-red T-shirt. "Krystal told me everything on our walk to school. I still can't believe it."

"Believe what?" Wendi stood and faced her new friends. "What's going on?"

"Last night I had a phone call." Krystal theatrically swept her palm across her forward. "And you'll never guess from who—LaShaun Penner!"

"Darlene Dittman's one-girl fan club?" Wendi asked in astonishment. "I didn't know you and LaShaun were friends."

"We're not! Practically the opposite. That's why I nearly freaked when I got her call!"

"What did LaShaun want?" Wendi asked.

"Just to give me some 'friendly' advice," Krystal said, flipping her wild blond ponytail over her shoulder and rolling her eyes. "What a crock! There wasn't anything friendly about her message. It was more of a warning—about the basketball cheer squad."

"Why does a football cheerleader care about the basketball squad?" Wendi asked as they left the fenced-in bicycle area and headed for the lockers.

Krystal grimaced. "LaShaun said she saw my name on the sign-up sheet, and she just wanted to save me from making a big mistake. According to LaShaun—which means Darlene, too—there's a rumor going around school that the basketball cheerleading squad is doomed. She said everyone's calling it the loser squad."

"Loser squad! That's ridiculous!" Wendi cried, outraged. "LaShaun is just trying to cause trouble."

"That's for sure," Anna grumbled.

"LaShaun said that a no-cut squad is for no-talent losers," Krystal added angrily.

"We're not losers! We have talent!" Wendi lifted her chin defiantly. "That's the lamest rumor I ever heard! LaShaun can't stop us from signing up."

"That's the spirit!" Anna rooted.

"That's why I told LaShaun to stuff it," Krystal said. "I pretended I was Madonna telling an annoying fan to bug off. Then I slammed the phone down hard on her."

Anna gave Krystal a high five. "Way to go, Krystal!"

"I would have loved to see LaShaun's face," Wendi said. "I'll bet she was really ticked off."

"I'm counting on it," Krystal said smugly.

"And she probably reported the whole thing to her pal Darlene," Wendi added with an amused grin.

"Speaking of Darlene, there she is *now!*" Anna declared, pointing toward a bank of lockers where two girls stood talking.

"But look who she's *with!*" Wendi exclaimed with horror. "Ohmygosh—it can't be, but it is! Darlene is talking to Tabby!"

Wendi stopped and just stared, too stunned to move. What was Tabby, her own best friend, doing with Darlene, the squad's worst enemy?

Glancing at Krystal and Anna, Wendi realized they were bothered by this, too. Krystal's blue eyes were narrowed, and Anna's usually smiling mouth formed a tense line.

"I bet Darlene is warning Tabby about the loser squad," Krystal said grimly.

"Tabby won't be fooled by a dumb rumor," Wendi said.

"I hope not." Krystal squared her shoulders. "Let's go find out."

Wendi bit her lower lip nervously and slowly began walking forward. "So here you are, Tabby," she said.

Krystal cut in, "We've been looking all over for you! Hope we aren't interrupting anything. . . . Oh, hello, Darlene." Krystal smiled, as if pleasantly surprised. "I didn't know you and Tabby were friends."

Darlene shrugged. "Not exactly."

"Then you must be asking Tabby's advice on your cheering technique," Krystal said with a wicked flash in her blue eyes. "Has Tabby been giving you tips on improving your hand motions?"

"No!" Darlene snapped, her milky skin turning a deep shade of scarlet.

Wendi covered her mouth so she wouldn't giggle. *Score one for Krystal,* she thought.

Darlene opened her mouth as if to make some nasty remark, but she seemed to change her mind and simply smiled. "My cheer moves are excellent. Isn't your name Coral or Christmas or something terribly cute?"

"Krystal. Which isn't nearly as cute as your 'darling' name."

Score two for Krystal, Wendi thought triumphantly.

Tabby looked as if she wanted to laugh. Instead, she said, "Darlene was just telling me a terrible rumor. Kids are calling the new cheerleading squad the loser squad."

"I wonder who would start a nasty rumor like

that . . . *Darlene*." Wendi paused and shot a dagger-filled gaze at the blond girl.

"I can't imagine." Darlene's expression was sugar-sweet innocence. "It's really too bad. Now no one will join the new squad. I guess if Coach Kendall really wants cheerleaders, the Castle Hill Cheerleaders could fit a few basketball games into its busy schedule."

"I think the basketball team wants its own squad," Tabby said, putting her hands on her hips. Wendi could tell that Tabby was steaming inside. More than anything, Tabby hated injustice and people who didn't play by the rules.

"You're wrong about no one joining the new squad," Krystal told Darlene. "There are at least four names on the list. Me, Anna, Krystal, and Wendi. But you already know that."

"*Me?*" Darlene tossed her pale-blond hair and pointed to herself. "I wouldn't waste my time checking out the sign-up sheet. The whole idea of two squads in the same school is lame. It's never going to happen."

"Why not?" Wendi asked indignantly, trying to keep cool. Blowing up and clobbering Darlene with her backpack wouldn't solve anything. Although it might feel good.

"There can't be a squad without cheerleaders. And I heard that Coach Kendall wants at least five girls or he'll forget the whole thing," Darlene said.

"Five will be easy to get," Anna said cheerfully. "We already have four. And the other girls who didn't make the football squad will be thrilled for another chance."

"You're forgetting that unfortunate rumor." Darlene gave a soft sigh and rubbed a smudge off her frosted plum-painted thumbnail. "None of those girls will show up. I'm sure of it. And really, it's for the best. It'll save you the embarrassment of being compared to our talented team. Our coach, my father, has big plans for us. His plumbing company is sponsoring our squad, getting great uniforms and funding us for important competitions. The Castle Hill Cheerleaders are destined to be big winners."

"Then you better work on your hand motions," Krystal snapped. "And something has to be done about LaShaun's timing. It stinks."

"At least I've got a squad to practice with." Darlene glared at Krystal. "It's too bad you didn't make our squad. But we only had room for the best cheerleaders."

Wendi burned inside. She was so mad she couldn't talk. But Tabby didn't have this problem.

"Krystal doesn't want to be on your stuck-up team, and neither do the rest of us!" Tabby fired back.

"We're glad we didn't make your squad," Anna said in a quiet, less sure of herself, tone.

"Our squad will make your squad look like limp rag dolls with bad timing and lousy hand motions," Krystal retorted.

"You don't have a squad. Five girls at least, remember? And I only see are four girls." Darlene's icy gaze swept over Wendi. "And one girl has geeky metal teeth that will blind everyone in the bleachers." Darlene flashed her own perfect, pearly smile. "Oh, there goes the warning bell. Gotta run. See you at the first football game. I'll be one of the girls holding pompons and cheering on the crowd. 'Bye!"

"That ... that ... that *witch!*" Wendi sputtered, staring at the retreating girl. Her hand went up to her lips and the words "geeky metal teeth" echoed painfully in her head.

"Darlene's just jealous," Anna said, patting Wendi's shoulder sympathetically.

"Well, she has a good reason to be jealous," Krystal said. "Because we're going to be the better squad. We'll be so good that the football team will beg our squad to cheer for *them.*"

"You said it, Krystal!" Tabby agreed.

Anna grinned. "We'll show that snooty Darlene and her friends!"

But Wendi wasn't so sure. If Darlene had been telling the truth about needing five girls to start a basketball squad, that could turn out to be a serious hurdle.

During her homeroom class with Miss Meyers, Wendi thought about this problem. She was dying to check Coach Kendall's sign-up sheet to see if any new names had been added. Unfortunately, there wouldn't be a chance to do this until lunch—and that was three periods away.

In Wendi's second period math class, instead of figuring out how to divide fractions, she started writing down the names of potential cheerleaders. She could remember some girls' names who hadn't made the Castle Hill Cheerleaders: Autumn Kulm, Meghan Wilkey, Brittany Ludwick, and Tanya Heinke. Even Darlene's nasty rumor about it being a loser squad couldn't keep all four from joining the new basketball squad.

By fourth-period English, Wendi was full of high hopes once more. She would become a cheerleader, be chosen for captain, and cheer her way to college scholarships. All her dreams would come true—and it would all begin with the new squad.

But when she and Tabby looked at the sign-up sheet during lunch break, all Wendi's hopes were sucked deep into a black hole. Only four names were listed. No one else had signed up. It was obvious that no one wanted to be on a loser squad.

Instead of being disappointed, Wendi gritted her teeth with determination. Somehow she'd convince Autumn, Meghan, Brittany, or Tanya to join the basketball squad. No way was she going to let Darlene beat them. A dumb rumor was not going to spoil her wonderful dreams.

Five

Wendi's determination had changed to disappointment by the end of the school day. She hadn't been able to talk to any of the four potential cheerleaders. Major depressing.

And instead of walking home with Tabby, Wendi was stuck researching an important report in the library. She had been so busy with her cheerleading dreams, she'd forgotten all about her country report. She'd been given Egypt to write about—a place she knew nothing about. And the report was due Friday in social studies and had to be at least five pages long.

And I haven't even written one page! Wendi thought in panic. She headed straight for the library, hoping other kids hadn't already checked out every book on Egypt.

Luckily, Wendi was able to find three books with lots of interesting pictures of pyramids, Egyptians, and fascinating gold statues. Ancient

Egyptian rituals, like strange ceremonies for the dead, sounded creepy and fascinating. Wendi kept on reading, her curiosity snared. And soon she was imagining herself living thousands of years ago.

After an hour, she had four rough pages. It wasn't perfect, but it was a good start. She figured if she worked hard, she'd be able to write another page at home before her friends came over to practice. Not that there was much use practicing for a squad that would probably never happen!

As Wendi left the building, a figure on the grassy school yard caught her attention. A slender girl with short, shiny black hair was spinning cartwheels like a whirling windmill.

Wendi's mouth dropped in astonishment when the girl jumped up, made a high V with her arms, swiveled her body, did a triple cartwheel, then catapulted up in a grand jeté and finished with a perfect split. Awesome!

The arm movements combined with tumbling spelled CHEERLEADER in capital letters. This girl knew her stuff. But she hadn't been at last month's cheerleading clinic. Wendi would have remembered her graceful style, athletic shape, and pretty hair. So who was she?

Wendi boosted her backpack high on her shoulders and hurried forward.

The black-haired girl must have heard Wendi's footsteps. She suddenly whirled around and stared hard at her.

"Hey! I want to talk to you!" Wendi called out, flashing a friendly smile and waving.

But the girl didn't smile or wave back. In fact, she resembled a frightened deer caught in bright headlights: trapped, afraid, panicked.

And before Wendi could reach her, the girl swooped down, grabbed her denim bag, then began to run—fast and far away from Wendi.

●●●●●●●●●●●

Six

Wendi didn't get a chance to tell Tabby, Krystal, and Anna about the strange girl until they met at her house that evening to practice cheers. They had already worked out for an hour and were taking a break, relaxing in Wendi's backyard.

"A mystery girl?" Krystal questioned, setting her lime soda on a wicker table.

"And you don't know her identity?" Tabby asked, leaning forward eagerly in a plastic lawn chair.

"I've never seen her before. She must have gone to a different elementary school or just moved here." Wendi sighed, feeling frustrated all over again. She was so close to being a cheerleader—but not close enough. "If I did know who she was, I'd pick up the phone right now and beg her to join our squad."

"We could really use her," Anna said as she

dipped a chip into salsa. "I checked with my brother. Darlene was right about Coach Kendall wanting at least five girls to start a new squad."

"And we only have four," Krystal said with a frown.

"Someone else is sure to sign up before Friday," Anna said optimistically.

"I hope so," Tabby said sounding worried. "Too bad the girl you saw ran off. I wonder what scared her away."

"Me!" Wendi exclaimed, slumping in her chair. "One look at me and *zoom*. She took off like I was a monster or a maniac. Which is so weird!"

"A real mystery," Tabby said, her green eyes sparkling with interest. "This reminds me of my favorite Julie Sutton book, *Vanishing Victim*. Maybe this girl faked her own death to get away from a crazed killer and she's hiding out in Castle Hill."

"Get real," Wendi scoffed. "Things like that don't really happen. Maybe to James Bond, but not to junior high kids."

"Why not?" Tabby retorted. "She might have witnessed a crime—maybe a murder! And she ran from you because she thought you recognized her. Her life could be in danger!"

"And Anna's always calling *me* dramatic," Krystal teased, her blond ponytail bouncing. "Tabby thinks she's Nancy Drew."

"No, I don't." Tabby blushed. "I don't drive a sports car, my father is a football coach not a lawyer, and I'd never go out with a guy named Ned."

"Who would?" Wendi joked, which made everyone laugh.

Tabby shrugged. "So I'm not Nancy Drew, but I do enjoy solving puzzles, and I have a pretty good memory—"

"More like *perfect* memory," Wendi said fondly, turning to Krystal and Anna. "Tabby is in the gifted program, and she's super smart. Sometimes she uses big words I've never heard of. And if she reads something, she never forgets it."

"Cool!" Krystal exclaimed. "I wish I had a perfect memory. It would help my career as an MTV star. I'd never forget my lyrics."

"I don't know much about rock stars or MTV," Tabby said. "But I'm really fascinated by puzzles: crosswords, cryptograms, cross sums—and now this mystery girl."

"She could save the new cheerleading squad," Wendi pointed out. "If she signed up, we'd have five girls. And she is really good. You should have seen her spin cartwheels. Wow! And the way she landed into the splits. What a gymnast! I bet she could teach us all some great moves."

"*If* we knew who she was," Krystal said.

"I can find out," Tabby said confidentially.

Wendi gave her friend a doubtful glance. "You can?"

"You bet!" Tabby grinned. "It's just basic investigative procedure. Ask questions, compile information, and reach a conclusion. If she goes to our school, I'll find her. Then I'll tell her about the basketball squad. She'll join. We'll make the five-girl minimum, and our problems will be over. Case solved."

"I'd be so glad if that really happens," Anna said.

"Me, too. I'll burst if I can't perform this year!" Krystal added, grabbing her pompons and waving them in the air. She jumped up and cheered, "Gimme an S! Gimme an O! Gimme an L-V-E! Solve! Solve the case, Tabby!"

"I'll do my best," Tabby said, her cheeks flushed with pleasure. Wendi could imagine her friend wearing a detective cloak and holding a magnifying glass. Once Tabby's brain started churning with a problem, there was no stopping her.

But reading a mystery wasn't the same as actually solving one. Wendi hoped Tabby didn't end up disappointed. "I'll do what I can to help," she told her friend. "But we should still talk to Meghan Wilkey, Autumn Kulm, Brittany Ludwick, and Tanya Heinke. They didn't make the Castle Hill Cheerleaders. Maybe they'll join our group."

"Great! The investigation will officially start tomorrow at school," Tabby declared.

"While you detectives are busy, I'll work on killing that dumb 'loser squad' rumor," Krystal said. "I know Darlene started it. She may be popular—but her kind of popularity is poison."

"Yeah," Anna agreed. "If it weren't for that rumor, lots of other girls would have signed up for the new squad."

Krystal nodded. "I just remembered that

Meghan and Autumn are in my math class. I can talk to them."

"Terrific!" Wendi said.

"Brittany and Tanya are in my gym class," Anna added. "I can talk to them."

"Super!" Krystal grinned and lifted her poms again. She jumped in place and motioned with her hands. "We'll F-I-G-H-T—Fight—Fight! To make our squad all right!"

Krystal and Tabby grabbed their poms, and they all started kicking and making up chants.

Wendi smiled at her friends, but she didn't join in the cheering. She leaned back in her chair, clasped her hands around her knees, and thought about the mystery girl. She was a talented gymnast, really flexible—but frightened. Wendi kept remembering that startled, panicked look on her face, like she'd been caught doing something wrong. But what could possibly be wrong about cartwheels, flips, and cheer moves?

What is going on? Wendi wondered. *I just wanted to talk with her. So why was she afraid? Why did she run from me?*

Wendi was still puzzling over these questions the following morning as she walked to school with Tabby. Walking took longer than riding bikes, but it gave them more time to talk. And they had plenty to talk about today.

"After you guys left last night, I played around with my computer and made you a printout on the mystery girl," Wendi said, handing Tabby a piece of paper. "I couldn't draw her picture, so I described her."

"Hey, this looks really professional." Tabby's green eyes sparkled as she smiled and looked at the computer printout. "This should help find her. Black eyes, about five foot two, athletic build, shiny black hair, carries a denim bag, purple sneakers ... Hey! Purple sneakers—now, that's a good clue."

"Yeah," Wendi said with a nod. "Not many kids wear purple shoes."

"I hope not," Tabby said. "We just have to find her." They paused at a corner and waited for a large truck to pass. "You know, I would never have gotten interested in cheerleading if it wasn't for you. But now I really want to be a cheerleader—more than ever."

"Why?" Wendi asked, giving Tabby a curious look as they crossed the street. "Did something happen?"

"Yeah. My dad called last night." Tabby's green eyes clouded over. "Of course, it was my brother he wanted to talk to. Dad is really proud that Adam's on the football team again this year. He's coming this weekend to watch Adam's first game. And I'm hoping to tell him I'm a cheerleader."

"By Saturday, we'll both be cheerleaders," Wendi assured her, understanding how much Tabby wanted to impress her father. Mr. Greene didn't visit often, and when he did, he spent nearly all his time with Adam. He often seemed to forget he had a daughter.

"It'll be cool to talk sports with Dad. Maybe

he'll even watch me cheer." Tabby ran her fingers through her wispy bangs. "So I really have to be on a cheerleading squad."

"Which means getting more girls," Wendi said.

"Especially your mystery girl." Tabby straightened her shoulders and glanced around. "I'll keep my eyes peeled for purple sneakers."

They slowed down as they entered the school grounds. Kids were everywhere: putting bikes away, standing around in groups just talking, or heading for their lockers. Classes didn't start for twenty minutes, so no one was in a big hurry.

"Let's go to the gym and see if anyone else signed up for our squad," Wendi suggested.

"I'm right behind you!" Tabby said.

But when they reached the far end of the gym and looked at the bulletin board, they both gasped.

Wendi's hand flew to her mouth and she cried, "Oh, no!"

"Who? Wh-Why?" Tabby exclaimed. "This is terrible!"

Wendi nodded numbly, staring at the sign-up paper. It was a mess. Someone had taken a black pen and put an ugly slash mark through all four of their names.

And at the bottom of the paper, two words were scrawled with the same poisonous pen: LOSER SQUAD.

● ● ● ● ● ● ● ● ● ● ●

Ševen

During lunch break, Wendi sat at an outdoor table with Tabby, Krystal, and Anna. A breeze raised goosebumps on Wendi's arms as she took the last bite of her peanut butter and kiwi jelly sandwich. She glanced up at the sky; the sun was only a shadow hidden by darkening clouds— fitting weather for her mood.

"Our sign-up sheet is ruined! How could someone be so mean?" Wendi asked for the third, fourth, or maybe hundredth time.

"Some people are real jerks," Tabby griped as she crumpled a Baggie and dropped it into her lunch sack.

"Yeah," Anna said, shoving her black bangs off her forehead. "I'm just glad someone posted a new sign-up sheet."

"A new sheet with the same old four names on it," Wendi said glumly. *"Ours."*

Frowning, she chewed her cookie. The chocolate chips could have been mud chips for all she noticed.

"I just know Darlene vandalized the list," Krystal said, her eyes narrowed with outrage. "She's a villain if I ever saw one."

Anna nodded and said, "Darlene looks like an angel, but she acts like a devil."

"Or maybe Darlene asked her hench-girl, La-Shaun, to mark up our list," Tabby said.

"Darlene has had a grudge against me since I criticized her hand motions," Krystal said, clenching her fists. "She's out for revenge. This is all my fault."

"Everything isn't about you," Anna said in a teasing tone that only a best friend could get away with. "If Darlene or LaShaun wrecked the sign-up paper, they did it to all of us." Anna's dark eyes clouded over. "Cheerleaders are supposed to have school spirit. But Darlene and La-Shaun are just mean-spirited."

"Well, they won," Wendi stated. "Everyone at school is talking about the loser squad—and no one wants to be part of it. We might as well put away our pompons and forget cheerleading."

"You can't mean that, Wendi!" Tabby objected. "It's not like you to give up so easily. Don't you want to compete in the nationals someday?"

"Of course. But it's never gonna happen now." Wendi sighed as she thought of the scrapbook tucked away under her bed. She'd bought it last month after tryouts. She wanted to have a cheerleading scrapbook like Valerie's, filled with newspaper clippings, competition photos, and award certificates. But it looked like her scrapbook would remain empty.

"Hey, we haven't lost yet!" Tabby suddenly slapped her palm on the table. "Everyone wipe off those gloomy faces! If we find one more cheerleader, we'll have our squad."

"But who?" Krystal asked, spreading her arms out in a questioning gesture.

"Wendi's mystery girl," Tabby said.

"But we don't even know her name, if she goes to this school, or if she wants to be a cheerleader," Wendi pointed out.

"Super sleuth Tabby is on the case," Tabby said with a confident grin. "I'll find her."

"Well, you'd better do it fast," Krystal said. "Because no one else wants to be on our squad. I asked Meghan, but she said no way. And Autumn said she'd just been offered an alternate spot on Darlene's squad."

"Darlene strikes again," Tabby grumbled.

Anna frowned. "I didn't have any luck either. Tanya is out sick. And when I asked Brittany to sign up with us, she just laughed. Like it was a big joke."

"Figures," Wendi said miserably. "Thanks to that rumor and now the vandalized sign-up sheet, everyone thinks our squad *is* a big joke."

"Well, it isn't!" Anna insisted. "We can't give up. That's one thing I've learned from Aunt Carlotta. She's still running her dance studio even though she's lost a lot of pupils to that fancy dance and exercise club Shape Up!"

"Tabby and I took some classes there last summer," Wendi said, surprised. "It *is* a really awesome place."

"I only take lessons with Aunt Carlotta," Anna said loyally.

"Me, too," Krystal added.

"Aunt Carlotta is a terrific teacher," Anna added. "Maybe she's a little behind the times, but she knows her stuff. And she's determined to make her business succeed—just like I'm determined to make our squad succeed."

"That's the S-P-I-R-I-T, Anna!" Krystal cheered. "If we refuse to give up, then no one can call us losers."

"We aren't losers," Wendi said firmly, taking the last sip from her milk carton. "The newest Castle Hill cheerleaders are going to be *winners.*"

"Then we'd better come up with a different title for our squad. Castle Hill is already taken by Darlene's crowd," Tabby said. "We'll have to call our squad something else."

"Castle Hill Basketball Cheerleaders?" Anna suggested.

"That's boring and long-winded," Krystal said. "We need a snappy, dramatic name."

"Not too dramatic," Anna argued. "Something simple and easy to remember."

"A spirited squad name," Tabby added.

"Let's see how our first squad meeting goes before we worry about a dramatic, easy-to-remember, spirited name," Wendi said.

Then she gritted her teeth, crossed her fingers, and hoped with all her heart that by Friday they had a squad to name.

● ● ● ● ● ● ● ● ● ● ●

Eight

Thursday after school, Tabby, Krystal, and Anna met at Wendi's house to practice. Despite the smiles, laughter, and teasing, Wendi could tell that her friends were as worried about Friday's squad meeting as she was. Tabby hadn't learned the mystery girl's identity, and no one else had signed the new basketball squad sheet.

Maybe Coach Kendall will settle for just four cheerleaders, Wendi thought optimistically. *Tabby, Krystal, Anna, and I work really well together. We don't need a fifth girl.*

After warming up and getting halfway through a basic "Get Up, Get Going" cheer, Wendi felt some splashes on her face and looked up at the darkening sky.

"Darn." She wiped her face and groaned. "It's not supposed to rain in September."

"Just what we don't need," Tabby griped, her light-brown braid swaying as she shivered.

"Oooh! I'm getting cold and *wet!*" Anna squealed, hugging her borrowed poms to her chest and bolting for the safety of the covered patio.

"Let's go inside!" Wendi suggested as rain began to shower down on them.

Practice ended before it had really started. Everyone's spirits were dampened—especially Wendi's. She had counted on this practice to sharpen their routine before the big meeting tomorrow. She wasn't even sure if Coach Kendall would expect them to try out for a no-cut squad, but Wendi liked to be prepared. If they didn't wow Coach Kendall with their four-girl routine, their first squad meeting could end up being their last.

Wendi slept uneasily that night and woke up feeling groggy and uptight. She stumbled out of bed and started to get ready for school. As she walked by her dresser mirror, a flash of silver made her stop to study her reflection. Decent figure, thick auburn hair, and nice gray eyes— but her silver teeth were the pits.

Why did her teeth have to be crooked? Why couldn't they be pearl white and straight? *I am a metal mouth,* Wendi thought bitterly. *No matter what Tabby or Mom say, my smile looks terrible.*

What would Coach Kendall think when he saw her glow-on-the-basketball-court teeth? Wendi would probably be the first girl in history to be cut from a no-cut squad. Wearing braces was definitely not something to cheer about.

Still, Wendi wanted to be a cheerleader more than anything. Besides, Tabby, Anna, and Krystal were counting on her. She wouldn't let them down.

When the final school bell rang that afternoon, Wendi met Tabby at their lockers. They shared nervous looks.

"I guess this is it," Wendi said as she took her knapsack containing shorts, a white T-shirt, sneakers, and pompons out of her locker. "We'll find out if we're going to have a squad or not."

"If we don't, it's all my fault for failing to track down the mystery girl." Tabby shook her head sadly. "She's a real enigma."

"Eni-*what?*" Wendi asked, amazed at Tabby's memory for unusual words. "An enema?"

"No!" Tabby burst out laughing. "No! Not an enema is . . . well, it's something completely different. I said an enigma, which means a puzzling mystery—which defines her exactly. I tried hard to find her, but no luck. I questioned nine black-haired girls. But none of them can do gymnastics or even owns a pair of purple shoes."

"Don't feel bad. We'll show Coach Kendall we don't need a fifth girl. Let's go in there and cheer our hearts out."

"Spoken like a true cheerleader," Tabby said with a grin. "I'm with you, Wendi."

Within minutes, Wendi, Tabby, Krystal, and Anna were gathered in the gym. While they waited for Coach Kendall to arrive, they did some warm-up stretches. Keeping active was easier than waiting, worrying, and wondering.

Coach Kendall came striding through the double metal doors a few minutes later. He was a short, wiry, twenty-something man with muscular arms and buzz-cut ash-brown hair. He introduced himself; then his gaze swept over the girls.

"I hope you know your stuff, because I'm new to cheerleading," Coach Kendall said. "My goal is to boost the moral of my boys."

Wendi exchanged a surprised look with Tabby. A cheerleading coach who didn't know anything about cheerleading? They were doomed!

Coach Kendall went on, "Basketball season is weeks away, so you will have plenty of time to come up with some inspiring chants. I don't expect fancy stunts or moves from you. Just jump around and yell loud and strong. Think you can cheer my boys on to win some games?"

Wendi nodded, but inside her mind was screaming with outrage. *No stunts! No fancy moves! Did Coach Kendall, like most of the school, think they were a bunch of losers?*

But Wendi kept her cool. A future squad captain did not blow up at her coach. "Uh, Coach Kendall. We can do lots more than just jumping and cheering. See, we've been working on a routine. Uh, would you like to see it now?"

He glanced at his watch. "Let's wait a few more minutes. Some other girls might show up."

"I don't think so," Krystal said slowly. "We're the only ones who signed up."

"Just four?" Coach Kendall frowned. "But I was told I needed five to have a solid squad."

"Who told you that?" Tabby blurted out.

"The Castle Hill Cheerleader's coach, Mr. Dittman. He was really helpful when I needed advice on starting my own cheerleading squad." Coach Kendall brushed his hand over his short bristly hair. "I don't like doing things halfway. Let's just call it quits."

"*No!*" all four girls cried in unison.

"We really want to be on your squad," Tabby said.

Anna nodded shyly.

"It doesn't matter how many of us there are," Wendi declared passionately. "We can cheer the basketball team on to victory."

"Think so?" Coach Kendall arched his eyebrow. "Well, I like your spirit. That's just what my boys need to push them to win. Go for it. Let's see what you can do."

Krystal squealed. Tabby grinned. Anna let out a relieved breath. And Wendi jumped forward to grab her pompons. Within seconds, music spilled out of Tabby's boom box.

All worries fled from Wendi's mind as the bouncy pop beat filled the gym. She took her place in line, lifted her hands high, then sprang forward with a cartwheel in unison with her friends. They began to chant the routine they'd practiced especially for the Knight's basketball team.

I love those Knights,
They're the team for me!
They have determination
To fight for victory!
They shoot, they pass, they dribble,
They fight with all their might.
We think this team is special,
And know they'll win tonight!

They ended the routine with double jumps, landing into splits. It was a simple routine with no stunts, aerials, or complicated moves. But it seemed to impress Coach Kendall. His enthusiastic applause was music to Wendi's ears.

"Well done! Just what I had in mind!" He grinned. "Maybe we *can* work something out."

Wendi and her friends gathered around Coach Kendall and awaited his verdict. Would their squad live or die?

"Hmmm . . . I still think we should have five girls," he began. "But I like your pep."

"So you'll let us cheer for the Knights?" Wendi asked hopefully.

"Not so fast. Since I also coach the soccer team, I'm awfully busy right now. I don't know the first thing about cheerleading, anyway. So you'll have to find an adult adviser *and* get a fifth girl. Do this by next Friday, and the squad is a go."

Coach Kendall waved, then turned and strode out of the gym.

*   *   *

"It's hopeless! We'll never find another girl!" Wendi complained as she left the gym with her friends.

"And an adviser!" Tabby groaned.

"Seven days isn't long enough," Krystal declared, swinging her tote bag as she walked.

"At least we're getting another chance," Anna pointed out.

"Anna's right," Tabby said. "We're lucky to get a second chance. And I know who would make a terrific adviser—the most perfect cheerleader in Castle Hill—Wendi's sister, Valerie."

"She's kind of busy," Wendi explained as they paused near the school library. "But I'll ask her."

"Great!" Krystal said. "Now what about a fifth girl? Tabby, any leads on the mystery girl?"

"Nobody knows who she is," Tabby admitted, sighing. "I'm beginning to think she isn't a CHJH student."

Wendi glanced around the school yard, her gaze sweeping out to the grassy back field. This was about the same time she'd spotted the black-haired girl several days ago. But the only people she saw out on the field were little kids playing soccer.

It was no use. The mystery girl would probably remain a mystery forever.

"Hey, look!" Tabby suddenly shouted, clutching Wendi's arm and pointing toward the library. "Purple sneakers!"

"You're kidding!" Wendi gasped, following Tabby's gaze and spotting a black-haired girl walking out of the library. She wore purple sneakers *and* carried a denim bag.

"What's up?" Anna asked, giving Tabby and Wendi a puzzled look.

Krystal raised her brows. "Since when are you two into fashion?"

"The sneakers have nothing to do with fashion! It *is* her!" Wendi exclaimed, jumping with excitement.

"*Her?* That black-haired girl?" Anna asked in astonishment.

"That's right. And we've got to talk to her!"

Anna shook her head firmly. "She can't be the mystery girl."

"Why not?" Wendi asked. "Do you know who she is?"

"Of course." Anna frowned. "Her name is Celine Jefferson and she's the new girl in my science class. But she's so rude and unfriendly that no one likes her. There's *no way* in the world she can be a cheerleader."

● ● ● ● ● ● ● ● ● ●

Nine

Anna and Krystal stayed behind while Wendi and Tabby hurried toward the black-haired girl.

"Celine!" Wendi called out, waving and running. "Wait up!"

The girl stopped in her tracks and whirled around. Surprise and a hint of fear crossed her face, but this time she didn't run away. Instead, she tightly gripped her denim bag and demanded suspiciously, "Wh-Who are you?"

"Wendi Holcroft," Wendi said, catching her breath. Tabby came up to stand beside her.

"Never heard of you." Celine narrowed her dark eyes at Wendi. "So how come you know my name?"

"My friend Anna told me." Wendi turned slightly and pointed back at Anna, who stood silently watching with Krystal. "Anna's in your science class."

"So? What do you want with me?" Celine asked

carefully, as if she were on trial and facing a hostile jury.

"Just to talk."

"I've got nothing to talk about with you guys. I really have to go. My grandmother is waiting."

"This will just take a sec," Wendi said quickly. "I saw you do some amazing moves a few days ago. You're a super gymnast."

Celine's expression turned to stone. "You must have seen someone else."

"With purple sneakers, shiny black hair, and a denim bag?" Wendi laughed. "Oh, it was you all right. You don't have to act modest. We think it's great you're so talented."

"I have no talent," Celine said firmly. "And I have no time to waste talking to girls I don't even know."

Wendi was puzzled by Celine's hostile tone. "Sorry, I forgot to introduce my friend Tabby. She's been working hard trying to find you."

Celine shrugged and scowled. "Am I supposed to care?"

"What's with the rude attitude?" Tabby snapped. "There's nothing embarrassing about spinning cartwheels and doing back flips. How long have you studied gymnastics?"

"I don't study *anything*," Celine said with a scowl.

"But your hand motions and cartwheels were so sharp and professional," Wendi insisted. "You've either had lots of training or you're a natural athlete."

"It doesn't matter." Celine shrugged again. "I really gotta go—"

"Wait! Don't you want to use your talents in a fun way?" Tabby cut in, standing in front of Celine so she couldn't leave. "Spin cartwheels, jump, kick, and show off your gymnastic skills?"

"We could really use your help," Wendi added. "We need one more girl so we can start a new cheerleading squad. And I could tell by your hand motions and gym moves that you've been a cheerleader before. Did you cheer in sixth grade?"

"No way!" Celine glared at Wendi. "You don't know what you're talking about."

"But I saw you," Wendi insisted.

"Then have your eyes checked!" Celine snapped. "I hate cheerleading. And most of all, I hate cheerleaders. So take your pompons and airhead attitude and leave me alone!"

"She was lying," Tabby told Wendi later that afternoon as they played Monopoly in Wendi's bedroom.

"Are we back to Celine again?" Wendi asked, leaning against a jumbo blue-striped pillow. "She made fools of us, and I'm sick of talking about her."

"But I've been replaying her words in my head, and I just realized something important," Tabby said, rolling a three and a five with the dice and landing on Marvin Gardens.

"Can't you just forget something for once in

your life?" Wendi sighed. "I made a mistake about Celine. The girl I saw doing cartwheels must have been someone else. End of story."

"No, this story is just beginning," Tabby said with a gleam in her hazel eyes. "Celine *has* been a cheerleader. I don't know why she lied to us, but she blew it when she mentioned pompons."

"Huh?" Wendi blinked. "What do you mean?"

"Remember when you first got me interested in cheerleading?"

"Yeah." Wendi smiled. "It took a lot of convincing, but you finally caved in."

"And I was surprised at how much skill it took to be a cheerleader. I loved using my dance training in such a fun way." Tabby leaned forward with a mischievous grin. "But you used to get really mad when I kept calling pompons 'pom-*poms.*'"

"Like the rest of the non-cheerleading world," Wendi said, rolling her eyes. "Everyone says it wrong ... oh! Now I get it. Celine said it the right way—pom*pons.*"

"Which proves she lied when she claimed to know nothing about cheerleading." Tabby rolled the dice again and landed on Park Place. "Celine is a bigger mystery than ever."

"Don't start with the hiding-out-from-criminals talk again," Wendi teased, passing Go and collecting $200. "I don't care about Celine. Anna was right when she said Celine was rude and unlikable. Cheerleaders are supposed to be friendly, not mean."

"You're forgetting Darlene and LaShaun."

"Well, *most* cheerleaders are super people. That counts Celine out big time. She could be the best gymnast since MaryLou Retton, but she's too mean to be a cheerleader."

"What if Celine's attitude is all a big act?" Tabby asked, pursing her lips as if ideas were racing through her head. "Maybe Celine acts obnoxious to hide a big secret."

"The only big secret I care about is how you got so good at Monopoly," Wendi joked as she paid Tabby $1,000 and the deed to Boardwalk.

"Simple strategy. The same sort of logical thinking that is going to solve the mystery of Celine." Tabby smiled confidently. "And this time I won't fail."

After Tabby left, Wendi tried to put cheerleading out of her mind. She offered to help her mother make homemade pizzas. Mrs. Holcroft's job as a financial consultant always seemed dull to Wendi, but her mom was lots of fun in the kitchen. Wendi loved it when they cooked together. And the pizzas turned out great!

Once her chores and homework were finished, Wendi went into her bedroom and sat at her computer. Making sure her door was shut securely, she accessed her top-secret, personal, keep-out-or-die-a-horrible-death journal by keying in her secret password, *"Pyramid."* She changed the password every week, taking no chances on a hacker-spy reading her private words.

Today I almost became a cheerleader. Almost is
definitely not good enough. I know my friends are
really bummed. Krystal says she'll explode if she can't
strut her stuff for an audience (her words, not mine).
Anna hid her disappointment with her usual cheerful smile. And all Tabby could talk about was Celine.
Tabby's obsessed—or maybe she's trying to keep
busy so she won't feel sad. Well, I can't lie to myself,
so I admit it. I'm sad, worried, and afraid my cheerleading dreams will never happen. Maybe I should
throw away my scrapbook. . . .

"No! I'm not giving up that easily," Wendi cried
softly. She hit Save and turned off her computer.

She remembered one thing she could do to help
save the new squad. They needed an adviser, and
she promised her friends she'd ask Valerie to take
the job. If only Valerie would just say yes. . . .

But thirty minutes later, Wendi was back in
her bedroom, disappointed again.

Valerie wanted to help. She would love to be
their adviser. And she felt terrible saying no. But
between going to school, studying, and working
part-time at a center for disabled kids, she had
no time to take on anything else.

Wendi had swallowed her misery and told Valerie she understood. Then she went to the phone
and called Tabby with the disappointing news.
She kept her voice calm, pretending she wasn't
upset. But once alone in her room, she flung herself on her bed and cried herself to sleep.

Ten

The next morning, Wendi was brushing her teeth when she heard a loud *ahooga* blast of a car horn. Mrs. Castle's car? What was it doing here? And so early!

Wendi hurried outside. In the car were Anna's aunt, Anna, Krystal, and Tabby.

"Good morning!" Mrs. Castle said as she stepped out of the driver's side.

"Hi! Are you going to be our fifth cheerleader?" Wendi joked.

"Heavens, no!"

Anna smiled through the open car window. "But my aunt is going to be an important part of our squad. I asked her to be our adviser, and she agreed."

Mrs. Castle touched her upswept dark hair. "If you'll have me. I usually teach ballroom dancing or ballet, so cheer moves will be a new experience for me."

"I think this is a great idea!" Wendi said enthusiastically. "Thanks, Mrs. Castle."

"Please call me Aunt Carlotta. With so many nieces and nephews, I'm used to that title," the older woman said. "But we didn't come over to chat in the driveway all morning."

"We're going to my aunt's place for cheerleading practice," Anna explained. "Wendi, can you come?"

"I think so. I'll run inside to clear it with my parents."

Wendi's parents agreed, and a short while later she sat beside her friends in the old-fashioned car that Anna's aunt called Archibald.

After an enjoyable ride, they arrived at Aunt Carlotta's Victorian-style mansion. It looked rundown from the outside, but the inside was attractive and comfortable. Aunt Carlotta led the girls to a basement room lined with a wall-length mirror and a barre for ballet.

"This used to be my dancing studio," Anna's aunt explained. "But when I opened my studio in town, I stopped using this room. I thought you girls might like to practice here."

"Super!" Krystal exclaimed as she danced a pirouette across the wooden floor.

"It'll sure beat getting rained out of my backyard," Wendi said.

"It's perfect!" Tabby said.

"I've always loved this studio." Anna grinned. "Although when I was little, I wasn't allowed to play here."

"That's because the steps are too steep and

dangerous for young children," Aunt Carlotta pointed out.

"So naturally Krystal and I made up stories about the studio," Anna added with a chuckle. "We pretended it was a dungeon."

"It'll always be a very special dungeon to me," Krystal said fondly. "I can't wait to cheer in here."

"So let's get moving," Wendi encouraged. "The newest Castle Hill cheerleaders need to practice."

"Then we'd better think of a different name for our squad," Tabby pointed out. "Our exact requirements were: a dramatic, easy-to-remember, spirited name."

"Like what?" Anna asked as her aunt crossed the room to turn on some music.

"How about Carlotta's Cheerleaders?" Krystal suggested.

Aunt Carlotta called out from the other side of the room, "I'm flattered, but no, thank you!"

All four girls chuckled.

"Maybe just Castle Cheerleaders," Tabby said.

"Still too much like Darlene's group," Wendi stated. "We need something unique and simple for our cheer squad."

"That's it!" Krystal exclaimed, grabbing Wendi's hands and jumping in place.

"What?" Wendi wrinkled her brow. "What did I say?"

"Our new squad name," Krystal replied. "Dramatic, easy to remember, and spirited: the Cheer Squad."

*   *   *

That night Wendi keyed into her computer journal:

Today we got an adviser like Coach Kendall wanted and got to practice in a real awesome dance studio. Fantastic! Anna is full of surprises, Krystal's energy is endless, and Tabby continues to be the best friend in the universe. And even though I still wish Valerie could have been our adviser, I'm thrilled with Aunt Carlotta.

This was the best day of my entire life. Even better than the time the tooth fairy accidentally left a $20 bill instead of just $1 under my pillow. And the best part was our new squad name. Today, the Cheer Squad was born.

● ● ● ● ● ● ● ● ● ● ●

Eleven

Monday during lunch, Krystal made a surprising announcement. And it had *nothing* to do with cheerleading. "I've entered the Harvest Festival talent show!"

"That's great," Wendi said with a smile. "I entered once with a gymnastic routine and came in third place."

"Well, I'm going to come in *first* place!" Krystal declared, her blue eyes sparkling. "And you'll never guess who's going to be my partner!"

"Not me," Anna said firmly. "I still haven't forgotten what happened when I helped you make that music video."

"My dad was able to fix his video camera," Krystal said as she took an apple out of her lunch sack.

"But it took a week for that purple dye to wash out of my hair!" Anna retorted.

"Sounds like performing with Krystal can be

hazardous to your health," Wendi said with a laugh.

"So who's your partner?" Tabby asked. "Maybe we should warn the unsuspecting girl."

"Not a girl . . . a boy. And a real hunk." Krystal grinned wickedly at Anna. "*Your* brother—and I don't mean seven-year-old Miguel."

"Esteban?" Anna nearly fell off her bench. "But he can't sing or dance. And he's too shy to get up in front of a crowd—unless it's at a basketball game."

"I'm helping Esteban get over his shyness," Krystal said. "And he doesn't have to sing or dance. He's going to play his guitar while *I* sing and dance. A retro sixties act. Together we'll make beautiful music."

Wendi took a bite of her tuna sandwich and thought, *I can tell Krystal really likes Esteban. And he must like her, too, or else he wouldn't be entering the talent contest.* Wendi gave a soft sigh and wondered if she'd ever find a boy worth liking. Of course, she couldn't expect a boy to like her back—not while her teeth were caked in geeky silver.

Krystal spent the next ten minutes describing her ideas for the talent contest: graceful ballet moves, the folk song she planned to sing, and costume ideas. Then she spotted Esteban walking away from the cafeteria and jumped up after him.

"There she goes," Anna said with a shake of her dark head. "Krystal has it bad. Last year we tried to avoid my brothers. Now Krystal's chasing after Esteban. She's nuts."

"Esteban *is* kind of cute," Wendi said, sipping her milk.

"Rufus is cute, too, but I don't want to date him," Tabby joked.

"Who's Rufus?" Anna questioned.

"My cat!" Wendi laughed. "You've probably seen him on his high throne—my fridge. Tabby isn't boy crazy yet, but she's crazy for cats—especially Rufus."

This started a whole conversation on pets. Aside from Rufus, Wendi had two parakeets named Paula and Katie (after two famous ex-cheerleaders). Anna had three dogs, a hamster, and an aquarium full of exotic fish. And though Tabby didn't have any pets due to her landlord's rules, she did have a scrapbook filled with cut out magazine photographs of animals she wished she owned.

Wendi could tell Tabby was starting to feel sad about not having a pet, so she changed the subject.

Leaning forward on the lunch table, she said, "I thought of someone else I can ask to join our squad—Rachel Steinberg from my science class. She's really nice and doesn't like Darlene's bossy attitude any more than we do."

"Sounds promising," Tabby said, giving a thumbs up. "You check with her, and I'll continue my investigation of Celine."

"Why are you bothering with *her?*" Anna asked in a disapproving tone.

"I think Celine was lying to us about hating cheerleaders," Tabby explained. "She's hiding a secret—something that's upsetting her. If I can help Celine with her problem, maybe she can help us by joining our squad."

"Rachel sounds nicer," Anna said. "Celine is too rude to be a cheerleader. Besides, you can't find out anything about Celine until she comes back to school. She wasn't in class today."

"Is she sick?" Tabby asked.

"Worse than that," Anna said ominously. "I overheard my homeroom teacher talking to another teacher, and they mentioned Celine's name."

Wendi shot Anna a curious look. "What did they say?"

"Just Celine's name and another word."

Tabby frowned. "What word?"

Anna paused, then answered in a hushed whisper, "Hospital."

"Just forget about Celine," Wendi told Tabby when they met at their lockers after school. "I'm sorry if she's sick, but there's nothing we can do."

"We could visit her in the hospital."

"She told us to leave her alone. She hates cheerleaders."

"Maybe her big secret is a deadly illness," Tabby said, putting two textbooks in her locker. "No wonder she was so rude. She probably only has a few months to live—or weeks!"

"I don't believe it," Wendi said firmly. "And you

wouldn't either if you'd seen Celine spin cartwheels. She looked athletic, not ailing."

"So then how comes she's in the hospital?"

"We don't know for sure that she's sick. She mentioned a grandmother. Maybe that who's in the hospital, and Celine is just visiting her," Wendi said, shutting her locker and slipping on her backpack. "Besides, we don't need Celine on our squad any more. Rachel will be our fifth girl—if her parents let her join. She thinks the loser squad rumor is a bunch of garbage."

"Good for her," Tabby said, her face lighting up.

Wendi smiled as they left their lockers. "Rachel may not spin cartwheels like Celine, but she's much nicer."

"That's for sure. But does she know any gymnastics or dance steps?"

"Not much, but she's willing to learn. And with her on our team, the Cheer Squad can be official."

"Cool!" Tabby said, jumping up.

Wendi's smile widened. "I can't wait to tell Krystal and Anna the good news!"

They turned a corner, and Tabby suddenly pointed. "We won't have to wait long. There they are, talking with . . . Yikes! Isn't that Darlene and LaShaun?"

"Yeah!" Wendi said. "Only they aren't just talking—they're arguing. And Krystal looks really mad. Let's go!"

Krystal's creamy skin was flushed a deep red, and her blue eyes glared like piercing lasers at Darlene. "I am not a big flirt!"

"I saw you myself," Darlene said coolly. "And so did LaShaun. You were all mushy over that conceited jock."

"Esteban is not conceited!" Krystal fired back.

"No way!" Anna cut in, stamping one foot. "He's *my* brother! And he's the best basketball player at our school."

Darlene nudged LaShaun. "Like anyone cares about basketball. The only serious sport is football."

"Yeah. No one cares about basketball," La-Shaun parroted, her shoulder-length jet-black hair styled in the same puffed, curled, and teased way as Darlene's ice-blond hair. She even spoke in the same sarcastic, sharp-edged way Darlene did.

"You're both dead wrong!" Tabby called out as she and Wendi hurried over. "Lots of kids care about basketball."

"Especially us," Wendi added.

"Cheerleader wannabees," Darlene said, rolling her eyes. "Don't you guys ever give up?"

"Never," Krystal said defiantly. "When we cheer the basketball team on to victory, those guys will become school stars. Then the football team will beg us to cheer for *them*."

"Dream on Coral, Christmas, or whatever your name is." Darlene lifted her chin and glared at Krystal. "And you don't care about the basketball team—you only care about one player. He's the only reason you're wasting your time waving pompons. You just want to show off in front of your boyfriend."

Krystal's face turned an even deeper crimson.

Anna quickly rushed to her friend's defense, "That's the dumbest lie I've ever heard."

"You've got no right to call her a liar," LaShaun lashed out. "Darlene just tells it like it is."

"According to her, maybe," Wendi said sarcastically. "But she's just afraid our squad will make you guys look bad—which is the truth."

Darlene started to laugh and LaShaun chimed in. "Oh, that's precious!" Darlene hooted. "As if your raggedy squad could ever compete with our group. I heard you guys don't even have matching uniforms or poms."

"Maybe not yet," Krystal snapped. "But at least our hand motions are smooth, not jerky."

Darlene glared at Krystal. "Well, we not only have matching pompons, but also matching uniforms, top of the line cheer shoes, and a professional trainer who has been a nationals competition judge."

"So what?" Wendi shrugged, acting like she didn't care. But in truth, she *was* impressed. Pompons, uniforms, shoes, and trainers were expensive. The Cheer Squad would have to hold lots of fund-raisers just to look decent.

"Anyone can buy fancy outfits, but you can't buy talent," Tabby said confidently. "And the Cheer Squad doesn't need to spend a penny for talent. We've got it naturally."

LaShaun raised her brows. "The Cheer Squad? What's that? A new TV sitcom?"

"Sounds nerdy to me," Darlene added with a haughty toss of her pale-blond head.

"For your information, that's the name of the new basketball cheerleaders," Wendi said proudly.

"A loser name for loser girls," Darlene sneered. "Come to our first game next week and watch *real* cheerleaders in action. You might just learn something."

"We'd just learn that your hand motions still stink and LaShaun still can't keep time with the music," Krystal said.

"Can so!" LaShaun cried.

"You girls are the ones who weren't good enough to be on our squad," Darlene said accusingly. "You're just a bunch of mismatched misfits."

"Even with mismatched pompons, we'll be a hundred times better than your squad," Wendi retorted.

Krystal blurted out, "And we can prove it!"

"We can?" Anna asked in surprise.

"How?" LaShaun questioned.

"Yeah," Darlene added. "There aren't any cheerleading competitions until spring. And that's months away."

"But there is the Harvest Festival talent show in two weeks," Krystal answered, her hands on her hips. "I dare you to enter."

"The Harvest Festival is too small-town for us," LaShaun boasted. "We wouldn't waste our time."

"Afraid to lose?" Krystal countered.

"Not on your life!" Darlene said furiously. "All right. It's a deal. The Castle Hill Cheerleaders against the Cheer Squad."

"You got it!" Krystal snapped. "And we'll show you who the better squad is."

"*Our squad,*" Darlene said smugly. Then she nodded at LaShaun, and both girls turned on their heels and strode off. The competition was on.

But Wendi was afraid this was more than a simple competition—it was an all-out *war.*

Twelve

That evening, Aunt Carlotta drove the new five-girl Cheer Squad to their first official practice.

Wendi enjoyed her second ride in the elegant old car, sitting back against the leather seat and half listening as Krystal told Aunt Carlotta and Rachel about the cheerleading challenge. The other half of Wendi's mind was visualizing cheer moves and deciding what sort of routine would win the talent contest—a prep cheer, a dance performance cheer, or maybe a routine with fun props.

We need a team captain to help make important decisions like this, Wendi thought as she stared out the window. *I hope someone nominates me. Maybe I should ask Tabby to—*

"Isn't this cool, Wendi?" Rachel asked suddenly.

"Huh?" Wendi blinked away her daydreams. "What?"

"This car!" Rachel's brown eyes shined. "I've never ridden in a classic before. Of course, I've never been a cheerleader before, either. I hope you don't regret asking me. I'm not much of an athlete."

"You'll do fine," Wendi assured her.

"None of us have been cheerleaders before. We'll learn together," Tabby said with a smile.

"But you've all had dance or gymnastic training. I've been taking saxophone lessons, which won't be of any help," Rachel said sounding worried.

"It'll help for belting out enthusiastic cheers," Anna said, turning to face them from the front seat. "You'll do great."

"Well . . ." Rachel still looked unsure. "I'll try not to let you down. I mean, I know I'm not cute and bubbly—the cheerleading type."

"That's an old-fashioned stereotype," Tabby stated.

"There is *no* cheerleading type," Wendi said firmly, "except friendly, dedicated, and athletic."

"But I'm not small boned and petite like you guys."

Krystal snorted from her front seat. She turned to face Rachel. "Who are you calling petite? Not five foot eight *me,* that's for sure. I couldn't be happier to have someone else as tall as me on the squad."

"We wouldn't even have a squad without a fifth girl," Anna added. "I'm so glad you joined us, Rachel."

*   *   *

A short time later, the Cheer Squad gathered in the "dungeon" dance studio.

Aunt Carlotta started off with a meeting. Wendi squatted on a mat between Tabby and Rachel, looking up at their adviser. Aunt Carlotta reigned like a queen on a corner of the balance beam, her ankles crossed elegantly, and her beige ballet slippers only inches off the ground.

"We have a lot of work ahead of us, girls," she began.

Wendi pulled a paper from her pocket, then raised her hand. "I made a list of things we need to do: our schedule, routines, outfits, fundraisers, and choosing a squad captain."

"Splendid!" Aunt Carlotta praised her, taking the paper. "You must have done this on a computer. I wish I were as organized as you. Thank you, Wendi."

Wendi smiled and hoped that she was a step closer to becoming squad captain. *Organized.* What a nice compliment.

"First off, we need to decide on a practice schedule," Aunt Carlotta said, setting Wendi's list aside. "I spoke with Coach Kendall, and he suggested two days a week. That doesn't seem like enough to me, though, so how about three?"

Five heads bobbed in agreement.

"So which three days?" Aunt Carlotta continued. "Since my dance studio business has slacked off, I have more free time than I know what to do with lately. I can pick you girls up any day after school."

"How about Mondays, Tuesdays, and Thursdays?" Tabby suggested.

Wendi, Krystal, and Anna nodded, but Rachel shook her head. "Not Tuesdays. I have sax lessons."

"How about Wednesdays?" Aunt Carlotta suggested.

"That should be okay. If my parents don't mind.'" Rachel fidgeted with her hands. "They don't really approve of cheerleading. They'd rather I join the school band. But they're pretty cool about letting me make my own decisions."

"If they need some extra convincing, you can have them call me," Aunt Carlotta said with a twinkle in her black eyes.

"Or they should look at Valerie's scrapbook," Anna said.

"Yeah," Tabby agreed. "Wendi's sister accomplished a lot with cheerleading. Her achievements would wow anyone."

"Not my parents," Rachel said with a frown. "They're into fine arts—museums, opera, and symphonies. They keep hoping I'll play my sax in a band."

"Creating music in a band isn't that different from creating excitement by cheering on a team." Krystal's blond ponytail swayed as she spoke enthusiastically. "Except cheering outfits are much cooler than band uniforms. And for a fashion accessory, I'll take pompons any day over a saxophone."

"You said it," Rachel agreed with a giggle. "The sax makes some great sounds, but it also makes my cheeks puff out like a chipmunk. Cheerleading is sounding better all the time."

"And it'll get even better," Aunt Carlotta stated with a mysterious smile. "I have some exciting news."

"News?" Krystal echoed.

"Yes," Aunt Carlotta said. "When I spoke to Coach Kendall, he said his soccer team was playing Belden Middle School this Saturday. I thought to myself, What a delightful chance to cheer in front of a live audience. So I told Coach Kendall you'd do it."

All five girls gasped.

"You didn't!" Anna and Krystal exclaimed in unison.

"We aren't ready!" Wendi objected.

"I'm definitely not ready!" Rachel whined. "I don't even know how to hold pom-poms—"

"Pom*pons*," Tabby corrected. "Named after a small variety of chrysanthemum."

"Whatever!" Rachel ran her fingers through her short, curly, chestnut hair. "I don't own any. And if I did, I wouldn't know how to hold them right!"

"You can borrow an old pair of my sister's," Wendi said.

"Thanks—but it's still too soon for me to perform in front of a real audience."

"Don't be silly," Aunt Carlotta said gently. "You'll all do fine. Consider this a rehearsal for the Harvest Festival."

"What about cheerleading outfits?" Wendi asked uneasily. She had a large collection of cheer supply magazines and knew the high-priced reality of cheering. Unfortunately, their team didn't have a rich sponsor like Coach Dittman.

"We can just wear white T-shirts and denim shorts," Tabby suggested.

"Splendid idea, Tabby," Aunt Carlotta said. "Simplicity is always a safe bet."

"But our pompons don't even match!" Wendi pointed out.

"Who cares?" Krystal said with a shrug. "We'll be unique and colorful."

"Mismatched, you mean," Wendi said, imagining the five of them looking like a crazy quilt on the soccer field. She glanced at her face in the wall mirror and saw a flash of silver. With her shiny silver teeth, she would be the most mismatched of all.

But Aunt Carlotta had confidence in them. And Wendi wanted to have confidence in her team and in herself. She'd been dreaming of cheering at a game since she was eight years old and watched Valerie kick, chant, and wave pompons for the first time. Valerie had looked so confident, radiant, and happy. And Wendi had resolved then that she wanted to be just like Valerie.

Maybe Saturday isn't too soon for the Cheer Squad's first performance, she decided. *If we work hard and practice a lot, we can wow the crowd. Then no one would dare call us the loser squad ever again.*

●●●●●●●●●●

Thirteen

When Wendi woke up the next morning, she was exhausted. Her muscles screamed for mercy when she climbed out of bed, and she noticed a yellow-purple bruise on her thigh where Rachel had accidentally kicked her. Getting ready for Saturday's game was turning into a *big* job.

They'd decided on a simple routine, a variation on one Valerie had done in sixth grade. It just involved clapping, chanting, and kicking—no fancy tumbling passes, props, or stunts. Anyone could perform this cheer. Well, almost anyone.

"Rachel is hopeless," Tabby complained as they walked to school. "I like her. Really I do. But she has the dancing ability of a three-legged gorilla."

"Poor Rachel," Wendi said, feeling a heaviness in her heart that outweighed the book-filled backpack on her shoulders. "She's trying so hard. But she needs weeks, maybe months, to learn basic steps. If only Rachel had some of Celine's talent."

"I wish!" Tabby sighed. "I dreamed about Celine last night. She was in a hospital bed, and instead of a pillow, her head rested on puffy pompons. I can't stop thinking about her—even when I'm sleeping."

"I'm too busy worrying about Saturday's soccer game to think about Celine," Wendi said, ducking to avoid a low-hanging willow limb. "We need more time to practice."

"Not tonight. Rachel has her sax lesson." Tabby frowned. "I still wish—"

"Not another word about Celine," Wendi cut in firmly. "She made her feelings clear. She doesn't like cheerleaders—and we don't like her."

Wendi headed for the outdoor lunch table when the bell for lunch rang. Tabby and Anna were already there.

"Hi, guys!" Wendi greeted, sitting down beside Tabby and spreading her lunch out. "Where's Krystal?"

"Where else?" Anna rolled her eyes. "With my brother. I'm glad they like each other, but I'm beginning to feel left out. If it wasn't for cheerleading practice, I'd hardly ever see Krystal."

"Don't feel bad," Tabby said. "You can hang out with us until she gets over her infatuation."

"Thanks." Anna unwrapped her triple-decker BLT. "Hey, guess who was back in class today? Celine."

"Celine!" Tabby cried.

"Yeah." Anna nodded, picking up her sandwich. "She was in class again—but her attitude stinks even worse than before. She came over and asked me if we ever got our fifth girl. I told her yes, and for a second I thought she looked disappointed."

"Maybe she changed her mind about being on our squad," Wendi said.

"I knew she was lying about hating cheerleading," Tabby added triumphantly.

"Oh, she wasn't lying," Anna said. "Because the next thing she said was, 'Cheerleading is just a rah-rah rip-off.' Then she hurried off like I was a bad disease she didn't want to catch. She's really got a grudge against cheerleaders."

"I wonder why," Tabby said, her gaze clouding over as if she was deep in thought.

Wendi shook her auburn head. "Oh, no. There Tabby goes again."

Tabby murmured, "Did a cheerleader do something mean to Celine at her last school? Or maybe she got cut from a squad unfairly." She rubbed her chin. "I'll burst if I don't discover Celine's secret."

Wendi frowned at her best friend. "There is *no* secret. We have plenty of other things to worry about, like the game on Saturday. Promise me you'll forget about Celine."

"Me? Forget something?" Tabby laughed, then grew serious. "You're right; our squad is more important. So from now on, I'll try to forget about Celine. But it won't be easy."

Tabby proved right about it not being easy. After school, as Tabby and Wendi left their lockers, they spotted a black-haired girl with golden skin hurrying through the school gates.

It was Celine.

"This is my chance!" Tabby exclaimed, walking faster and forcing Wendi to run to keep up with her.

"Chance for what?" Wendi demanded. "Where do you think you're going? Our homes are in the opposite direction?"

"I'm going to follow Celine. I want to find out where she lives. I want to know why she hates cheerleaders. And this is my chance to find out." Tabby paused and gave Wendi a sharp look. "Are you with me or not?"

Wendi almost said, "Not"—but the intense, determined expression on Tabby's face stopped her. They were friends, after all. Best friends, which meant a lot to Wendi. So she just nodded and answered, "I'm with you, Sherlock. Lead the way."

Celine moved quickly, hurrying past groups of kids, never glancing or talking to anyone. She seemed intent on reaching her destination—wherever it was. And a safe distance behind, Wendi and Tabby followed.

"This is crazy," Wendi said through rapid breaths.

"I know." Tabby grinned mischievously. "But it's fun and exciting. And maybe we'll find out something important about Celine. Look! She's making a right turn. Come on!"

Wendi paused, catching her breath by leaning against a stop sign. Then she hurried to catch up with Tabby. They were entering an area of older homes with small yards decorated with brick planters, tidy gardens, and neatly manicured hedges.

Celine opened the chain-link gate of a pink-and-green house, then walked up the cement entryway. As she reached the porch, a small, tawny-skinned woman with silver-streaked black hair stepped from the house and hugged her.

Wendi and Tabby quickly ducked behind a dense oleander bush. "That woman resembles Celine," Tabby whispered. "It must be her mother."

"Maybe. But she looks older than our mothers," Wendi said, crouching down and glancing around to make sure no one was watching *them*. They must have looked silly, carrying backpacks and skulking down in the bushes like curious chipmunks. Wendi was beginning to *feel* silly, too.

"She could be Celine's aunt or grandmother," Tabby guessed. "I wonder if she was the person in a hospital."

"Well, it doesn't look like anybody's in a hospital now, and I don't like spying." Wendi pulled Tabby by the arm. "We found out where Celine lives. So let's go."

"Not yet," Tabby said, shaking her head. "Get a look at Celine's face. She's smiling and laughing at something the older woman said."

"So?" Wendi asked with a shrug.

"It proves Celine isn't always nasty and rude. She's even pretty when she smiles."

"The older lady is going into the house." Wendi

perked up and pointed through the bushes. "But Celine is just standing there."

"Not standing. She's sitting on the porch and reaching into her backpack," Tabby observed.

"And taking something out. Probably school books," Wendi said. "Maybe she's going to do her homework."

"Not books. Something purple and silver, like a balled up sweater or shirt." Tabby suddenly gripped Wendi's arm. "Oh, my! I can't believe it!"

"I can't either!" Wendi exclaimed, covering her mouth with her hand. "But I'm seeing it with my own eyes, so it must be true."

"It *is* true!" Tabby declared triumphantly. "Celine, the cheerleader hater, owns a set of pompons!"

● ● ● ● ● ● ● ● ● ● ●

Fourteen

That evening, Wendi played solitaire on her computer, but it was hard to concentrate. She kept thinking about Celine's strange behavior earlier. Celine had actually swished her purple and silver poms and performed a short cheer for a team called the Matadors.

But I've never heard of that team, Wendi thought, puzzled. *Is it a real team or something Celine just made up? And if Celine hates cheerleaders so much, why did she chant cheers in her yard? Weird.*

Tabby was right about Celine being mysterious. Something strange was definitely going on. But what?

Whenever Wendi was confused, it helped to sort through her thoughts by recording them in her journal. So she keyed her secret code word and accessed her computer journal.

Today Tabby and I saw Celine waving a set of pompons. Tabby wanted to run right over and confront her but I said no. Why talk to someone who doesn't want to talk to us? Celine would just say something rude again. No thanks. So Tabby and I went to my house instead. We did our homework, played with Rufus, and goofed off with tumbling moves and funky steps to music from Tabby's boom box. Valerie even interrupted her studying to do some cheers with us. It was fun, and we laughed a lot. Too bad Anna, Krystal, and Rachel didn't practice with us. Our routine still needs a lot of work. And the soccer game is just four days away . . . much too soon!

After school the next day, the Cheer Squad practiced at Aunt Carlotta's mansion. Although no one had mentioned choosing a squad captain, Wendi stepped unofficially into the role. She helped Rachel spring into cartwheels, and she gave Tabby some tips on smoother back flips. She even tried to boost Anna's confidence by complimenting her a lot.

But Wendi didn't know what to do about Krystal. Krystal had all the steps down perfectly, but she kicked higher and cheered louder than anyone else. She acted like she was *the star*. She blew the rhythm of the whole squad.

But how do you tell someone to tone it down without getting them ticked off? Wendi wondered. *You can't.* So Wendi bit her lip and said nothing.

But by Thursday's practice, her lip was numb, and her frustration was mounting. *Krystal is showing off worse than ever,* Wendi thought with annoyance. *It's obvious that her movements are out of sync with everyone else. So why doesn't someone say something?*

But no one did. Maybe they didn't notice. Or, more likely, they were too busy trying to remember hand motions, dance steps, the words to the "Go-Fight-Win" chant.

If I were squad captain, it would be my duty to tell Krystal to cool it with the exaggerated moves, Wendi thought. *But I'm not the captain. No one is . . . yet.*

By the end of practice, everyone had the moves down to the "Go-Fight-Win" cheer, and they were ready for the soccer game. Well, almost. Wendi suggested they meet again Friday night to practice one last time. But Aunt Carlotta had dance lessons scheduled at her studio, and Rachel's parents were taking her to a play.

So the next time they got together would be at the soccer game—the first public appearance of the Cheer Squad.

Wendi slipped on her white T-shirt and denim shorts Saturday morning and made a *big* decision. Her conscience wouldn't let her keep quiet any longer. Someone had to warn Krystal not to show off at the game. And in future-squad-captain style, Wendi appointed herself to the job.

Wendi enjoyed a breakfast of French toast and fresh fruit with her parents. They had a lunch date with some friends, so they couldn't come to watch Wendi cheer, although they promised to come next time. And Mr. Holcroft was happy to drop Wendi off at the junior high.

Wendi saw Aunt Carlotta first. The squad adviser sat on a bench next to a cooler of cold drinks and snacks. Then Wendi spotted her four Cheer Squad friends. They were gathered on the green soccer field, wearing T-shirts, shorts, and holding mismatched pompons.

As Wendi joined her friends, she shivered. Gray clouds blocked the sun, and the grass was damp with dew.

"Are you nervous?" Tabby asked.

"A little." Wendi nodded, watching people fill into the bleachers. "Meganervous. But excited, too. All those people will be watching us."

"Mostly they'll be watching the soccer players," Tabby pointed out.

"But during the break, we'll be center field." Wendi smiled. "I've been dreaming about being a cheerleader for years, and now I am. It's wonderful and terrifying at the same time. Of course, I never dreamed it would be so cold and damp. Brrrr!"

"It *is* chilly," Tabby agreed, hugging herself to keep warm. "Most of the spectators have jackets."

"I wish *we* did," Anna said, coming over with Krystal and Rachel. "I have goose bumps all over my arms. And the grass is wet. We'll be doing cheers with soggy sneakers."

"It rained last night," Rachel put in. "Maybe

it'll rain again, and the game will be canceled. Then we can practice more before our first game."

"We don't need any more practicing. We'll do super!" Krystal said confidently. "How can we miss? We're the Cheer Squad—Gimme a C! Gimme an H! Gimme an E-E-R! Yay, Cheer Squad!" She jumped high, kicked, and swished her pompons.

Everyone laughed—except Wendi.

Krystal is way too dramatic, Wendi thought uneasily. *I have to tell her. It's now or never.*

She took a deep breath, grabbed on to what courage she could summon up, and asked Krystal for a private talk. When they reached the side of the bleachers, Krystal gave Wendi a curious look.

"So what's up? Do you have a problem?"

"Not me, exactly. . . ." Wendi's words trailed off and she stared at her damp, grass-stained sneakers. "Uh . . . You know I think you're a terrific cheerleader."

"Thanks." Krystal grinned. "I think you're good, too."

"But maybe you're maybe *too* terrific." Wendi paused again. This was harder than she'd expected. "I don't want you to be embarrassed today, so I felt I had to tell you the truth."

Krystal's grin faded. "What truth?"

"You kick higher and yell louder than the rest of us."

"So what?"

"Your moves are exaggerated. It's like you're trying to show off. Be the star cheerleader."

"What's wrong with that?" Krystal said defensively. "I'm doing my very best."

"Your best is too much. Relax a little."

"But I want to shine and wow the audience. I've studied gym and dance since I could walk. Performing is my life."

"And cheerleading is really important to *me*." Wendi frowned. "But it's a team sport. We all need to work together. You've gotta stop acting like a prima donna."

"I am *not* a prima donna!" Krystal cried, her blue eyes blazing with outrage. "But if you want me to relax—fine. I'll relax. And you'll be sorry."

With a toss of her blond ponytail, Krystal whirled around and went back to Anna, Tabby, and Rachel.

Wendi sighed, already feeling sorry. This had definitely not gone well. *Being a squad captain might be a bigger responsibility than I want,* she thought. *But if Krystal stops grandstanding, then it will be worth it.*

A short time later, Coach Kendall blew the whistle, and the soccer game began. Wild yells, hoots, and whistles filled the air as Castle Hill Junior High took on Belden Middle School. The Cheer Squad jumped and waved their poms enthusiastically. Wendi felt jazzed and ready to raise some spirit when a time-out was called.

"We're on!" Aunt Carlotta declared.

An electric thrill shot through Wendi when Coach Kendall introduced the Cheer Squad. She was really and truly a cheerleader. In the future, when she competed in the nationals, she would always remember this first cheerleading moment.

"Positions," Aunt Carlotta told them. "Poms up for the "Go-Fight-Win" cheer."

Wendi raised her poms in the high V position— and felt light splashes on her face and arms. She shared an alarmed look with Tabby. Had they gotten this far only to be rained out?

As quickly as the sprinkles started, they stopped. Then Aunt Carlotta started their music—and the Cheer Squad was *on!*

> *We're with you, Castle Hill, so* go!
> *We're with you, Castle Hill, so* fight!
> *We know you can do it.*
> *We know you can* win!
> *So Castle Hill* Go-Fight-Win!

The first run through, the chant went perfectly. And Wendi noticed with relief that Krystal wasn't showing off. No overly high kicks or thundering yells . . . in fact, Wendi could barely hear Krystal at all.

But when they repeated the cheer, Wendi realized that Krystal was moving like a limp puppet. And she could sense the others were aware of this, too. Anna seemed rattled, once clapping when she was supposed to kick. And Rachel, who had started out awkward, grew even worse.

Wendi tried to perform the best she could, but she was so busy watching Krystal, she had a hard time concentrating. So she forced herself to look away—and that's when she saw her blond enemy grinning at her from the bleachers.

Darlene Dittman was there! And probably cracking jokes about the metal-mouthed cheerleader.

Wendi's smile faded, and when she cartwheeled forward, her foot hit a wet spot. She flew upward, then crashed into Rachel, and landed in a patch of mud.

Rachel screamed, her arms flailed wildly, and she stumbled against Anna and Krystal. Two more cheerleaders down. Only Tabby was left standing, staring in horror at her friends.

But the real horror was discovered moments later—when Rachel tried to stand up and *couldn't.*

"My ankle!" Rachel sobbed, huge tears of pain streaming down her mud-speckled cheeks. "It hurts so much! Oh, no! I think it's broken!"

Fifteen

"How's Rachel?" Wendi asked, looking up anxiously as Aunt Carlotta stepped into the living room of Castle Mansion. Aunt Carlotta had just gotten off the phone with Rachel's mother, and Wendi, Tabby, and Anna waited nervously for the results. The disastrous soccer game had been over for hours—but the Cheer Squad's worries had only grown worse.

"Is her leg broken?" Tabby asked, leaning forward on the couch with her hands clasped.

"No," Aunt Carlotta answered, looking weary as she sank in a high-backed Victorian chair. "But Rachel's ankle is sprained. She'll have to take it easy for a while."

"I'm glad it's only a sprain," Anna said with relief. "I'll call Krystal right away with the news. I know she's worried, too. I'm surprised she wanted to go home rather than wait here with us."

I'm not surprised, Wendi thought with a bitter twinge of guilt. *Krystal is angry with me. And I can't blame her. If I hadn't insulted her, we wouldn't have fallen down in the muddy grass like a bunch of demented dominos. And Rachel wouldn't have gotten hurt.*

"At least Rachel won't have to wear a cast," Anna rattled on. "In fifth grade, I had to wear one for two months on my arm, and it was the pits. Really uncomfortable. Especially when I had an itch."

Aunt Carlotta was the only one who smiled at Anna's attempt to lighten the mood. Wendi felt too guilty, and Tabby stared off in space as if her thoughts were somewhere else.

"Chin up, girls," Aunt Carlotta said brightly. "We may have had a small setback, but the Cheer Squad will come through with flying colors at the Harvest Festival."

Wendi cringed at the idea of cheering in public again. She wanted to hide her face in a paper bag—not compete in a talent contest they were sure to lose.

"We're not ready for the Harvest Festival," Wendi said. "Today was worse than a small setback. It was a mud-pie disaster."

"Our soccer team won," Anna pointed out cheerfully.

"Only because the opposing team couldn't stop laughing at us," Wendi replied. "I've never been so embarrassed!"

Tabby snapped out of her daydreams and gave Wendi a startled look. "We were all embarrassed, but it's over. We'll do better next time. Especially if . . . well . . . if something works out."

Wendi gave Tabby a sharp, suspicious glance. What was Sherlock Tabitha plotting now?

"I have confidence in you girls. Everything will work out perfectly fine," Aunt Carlotta said.

"We're laughingstocks," Wendi griped. "Our soccer team may have won, but the Cheer Squad lost big time. I dread going back to school on Monday."

"If we just act normal, it'll be okay," Anna said, giving Wendi an encouraging smile. "Everyone makes mistakes."

"But this mistake"—*my mistake,* Wendi thought—"caused Rachel to get hurt."

"Poor Rachel," Anna said. "I hope she's not in too much pain."

"I wonder if she'll be able to go to school," Tabby said thoughtfully. "Maybe she'll use crutches."

Wendi sighed. "Rachel won't be able to cheer for weeks, maybe months."

Aunt Carlotta tapped on the coffee table with her fingers and gave them a no-nonsense look. "I want to see a positive attitude from you girls. I'm sorry about Rachel, too, but the Cheer Squad has to go on. This isn't a funeral."

"Well, it might as well be," Wendi insisted. "Without five girls, we don't have a squad. And with Rachel injured, we only have four girls. The Cheer Squad *is* dead."

Wendi sulked in her bedroom for the rest of the weekend. Tabby called and invited her to a matinee, but she wasn't in the mood for fun. When Tabby pressed her for a reason, Wendi reluctantly explained about her talk with Krystal. Tabby assured her that she'd done the right thing, but that didn't help make her feel any better.

Wendi's parents noticed her down mood and tried to lure her out of her room with offers of Chinese food and a visit to the computer store. Wendi was tempted—but she couldn't shake her sense of guilt. The Cheer Squad had messed up big time, Rachel had a sprained ankle, and Krystal was still mad at her.

It's all my fault, Wendi thought as she fell into a troubled sleep Sunday night.

And she was still miserable Monday morning as she walked to school.

"Wipe off the gloomy face," Tabby ordered.

"I can't," Wendi said, stubbing her toe against an exposed root in the sidewalk. "Ouch! I can't even walk straight. My whole life is the pits."

"You're starting to sound as dramatic as Krystal."

"Don't mention *her* name. If I hadn't called her a prima donna, none of this would have happened. I'm not the squad captain. I had no right to criticize her cheerleading."

"You had the guts to do something when no one else did," Tabby said. "I'm proud of you. It's great how you care so much for the squad."

"Maybe I care *too* much." Wendi pushed an auburn strand of her hair from her eyes. "If I didn't have such huge hopes for the Cheer Squad, I wouldn't be so bummed. I expected too much."

"It's good to have dreams. I keep dreaming that someday I'll impress my dad. We both have to hold onto our dreams. Besides, the Cheer Squad still has a chance to succeed." Tabby gave Wendi a mysterious smile as they paused at an intersection, "I've been thinking about something . . . someone . . . and I may be able solve our problems."

"Not Celine again!" Wendi protested.

"Purple shoes, purple pompons, and a team called the Matadors intrigue me. But I'm not revealing my theory until I've made an important call to San Jose."

"San Jose? Who do you know there?"

"No one—yet." Tabby chuckled, then cut off suddenly as they reached the school parking lot. "Oh, no! Don't look now, but there's Darlene and LaShaun."

Wendi groaned. "The two last people in the world I want to see."

"Too late! They've spotted us," Tabby cried. "And they're coming our way!"

Monday, 7:57 P.M.

Practice was canceled tonight. Aunt Carlotta had a business meeting. There was no point practicing anyway. I can still hear Darlene's snotty words: "I just loved your funny routine. LaShaun and I laughed for hours. You should change your team name from the Cheer Squad to the Clown Squad."

Darlene is such a witch! I wanted to wrestle her to the ground and show her how yucky mud feels. Then she said she couldn't wait to see the Cheer Squad perform at the talent contest. "Maybe there's a special award for funniest act. Then the Cheer Squad won't be total losers. Of course, our squad will take first place."

Wendi frowned, pausing with her fingers resting against the computer's keyboard, and wondered if the talent contest would turn into another disaster. Sighing, she continued typing.

Maybe we should drop out of the talent contest. Why take the chance on more embarrassment? Besides, Krystal's still mad at me, Tabby is busy with her secret mission, and Rachel wasn't even at school today. So everything is a huge mess. And I never did become squad captain—but I've decided to do one final, captainlike thing. Tomorrow at lunch I'll call a meeting of the Cheer Squad.

At lunch the next day, Wendi tapped her foot and glanced at her watch. Ten minutes had passed. Anna, Krystal, and even Rachel—who walked with crutches—had arrived. But no Tabby.

"Where is she?" Wendi muttered.

"Maybe she's inside the cafeteria buying a hot lunch," Anna said as she unwrapped a huge tripledecker sandwich. For a petite girl, Anna could really put away a lot of food.

"Tabby always brings her lunch." Wendi glanced at her own unopened sack lunch. She was too nervous to eat.

"Maybe Tabby forgot about this meeting," Rachel said, her crutches propped against the wooden table.

"Tabby never forgets anything," Krystal scoffed. "She probably just had something better to do. Which isn't such a bad idea." She shot Wendi a hostile glance. "I'm not that crazy about being here myself."

"Well, I'm glad you came," Wendi said sincerely. It hurt when one of her friends was angry with her. "I never should have criticized you, Krystal. I'm sorry."

Krystal's blue eyes widened with surprise, then clouded with a darker emotion, maybe guilt. "It's okay."

"Hurray!" Anna applauded. "I'm so glad you two are making up."

"Why were you fighting, anyway?" Rachel wanted to know.

Wendi and Krystal's gazes met, and slowly they both smiled.

"It's not important now," Krystal said, pushing back her blond bangs. "Let's just get on with this meeting. We can fill Tabby in later."

"All right." Wendi took a deep breath. "I'll just get to the point. I take cheerleading seriously and don't like doing things halfway, like competing in a talent show when we aren't ready. So I think we should drop out of the competition."

"And let Darlene the dirtbag win?" Krystal demanded.

"Her squad will probably win anyway," Wendi said.

"Don't quit because of me," Rachel said firmly. "You guys cheer really well together. I know you can win the contest."

"And in a few weeks, Rachel will be able to cheer with us again," Anna said brightly.

"We gotta be realistic." Wendi frowned, hearing Darlene's voice taunt "Clown Squad" over and over in her mind. "Everyone is laughing at us. Darlene spread the rumor about us being the loser squad, and then we stumbled in the mud. No one will take us seriously."

"All because of my prima donna attitude." Krystal hung her head miserably. "I wrecked this for everyone. Wendi was right to lay into me for showing off. I was trying to be the star instead of part of a team. I shouldn't have blamed Wendi for being honest with me."

"Only an adviser or squad captain has the right to criticize you," Wendi said.

"But Aunt Carlotta hadn't noticed, so you were right to speak up. I'm the one who messed up the routine to get even. I threw everyone's rhythm off."

"My rhythm was off to begin with," Rachel admitted. "I was a klutz to fall down and sprain my dumb ankle."

"I fell down with you," Anna said sadly. "I'm sorry about your ankle."

"I'm more sorry," Wendi said. "I caused you

both to fall down when I saw Darlene in the bleachers, and I knew she was making fun of my braces."

"Listen to us!" Krystal said, starting to giggle. "We're arguing over who's to blame."

Anna giggled, too. And Rachel joined in.

Wendi stared in amazement at her friends. It was crazy! They had made fools of themselves at the soccer game. Their squad was in trouble. They were miserable. And yet they were laughing . . . so she burst out laughing, too.

Finally, Wendi wiped tears from her eyes and managed to calm down. "We really should take a vote."

"On who's to blame the most?" Krystal joked, cracking up all over again.

"No." Wendi regarded her three friends solemnly. "On whether to drop out of the talent show."

Anna sniffled. "Maybe you're right."

Wendi slapped her hand on the table like it was a judge's gavel. "All in favor of canceling before anyone else breaks her ankle or falls down in the mud, say aye."

Anna and Krystal shared an uncertain look. Then Krystal sighed. "Aye."

"Me, too. I guess," Anna said. "Aye."

"I can't cheer anyway for a while," Rachel said, bending down to touch her bandaged ankle. "Aye."

Wendi inhaled sharply, hating to utter the word. She hated to let Darlene's squad win. But mostly she hated to be a quitter. And she could actually feel her heart breaking.

"Aye." She let out a long, shaky breath. "Four votes . . . motion carried. The Cheer Squad is officially—"

"*No!*" someone interrupted.

Wendi whirled around and saw Tabby coming forward—and she wasn't alone.

"The motion is *not* carried. It's not unanimous because I vote nay," Tabby exclaimed with a huge grin. "And I think the newest member of the Cheer Squad will vote with me." She gestured to the black-haired girl standing beside her. "I think you already know Celine Jefferson—but there are things you don't know *about* her. Listen up and I'll tell you."

●●●●●●●●●●●

Sixteen

Wendi couldn't take her gaze off Celine. The mystery girl was *here*. And she actually wanted to become a cheerleader. Incredible!

"Sit down and fill us in," Krystal said eagerly, scooting closer to Anna to make room.

Anna turned her head and gave Celine a suspicious look. "I thought you hated cheerleaders."

Celine clasped her hands on the table, her silky black hair falling across her brow. "I just said that so you'd get off my case. Besides, it was easier than the truth."

"What truth?" Wendi asked.

"It's hard to talk about." Celine pushed back her hair and bit her lip. "Tabby can explain."

Wendi reached across the table and poked Tabby. "So go ahead. Explain!"

Tabby flashed the proud smile of a detective basking in a solved case. "As Wendi knows, I've been curious about Celine from the beginning."

"Obsessed," Wendi teased.

"Well, it didn't make sense for Celine to excel at cheerleading and yet say she hated cheerleaders. I knew she was new to our school, so I wondered if she'd been a cheerleader at her last school."

"You were right," Celine said quietly. "But I can't believe you bothered with me after I was so mean."

"You were mean because you were afraid," Tabby said. "Anyway, when I learned that Celine had purple and silver pompons and knew a cheer for a team called the Matadors, I remembered an article in a cheerleading magazine."

"An article that was three months old. You sure have a good memory!" Celine marveled at the idea.

Wendi chuckled. Celine had a lot to learn about Tabby.

"Not many schools have purple and silver as their colors and a team called the Matadors," Tabby said. "So I checked my magazine and found the article. It was about a cheerleading tragedy in San Jose."

Wendi saw Celine's face go pale.

"The sixth grade cheerleaders from Leland School were returning from cheerleading camp," Tabby continued.

"We won some awards and had a great time," Celine added solemnly. Wendi thought she saw tears in Celine's dark eyes. "Mom was so proud of me. She even sang songs and yelled cheers

with us girls on the way home, until the bus—"
Celine broke off with a soft sob.

Tabby patted Celine's shoulder. "There was an
accident. A truck ran a light and swerved into
the bus, causing the bus to tumble into a ditch.
No one was killed, but there were some serious
injuries. Broken bones, a girl was paralyzed,
and—"

"My mom is still in a coma," Celine said sadly.
"She enjoyed my cheering so much—but because
of it, she might never wake up. It's all my fault."

"No, it isn't," Tabby said firmly. "We already
talked about this, and you agreed to stop blam-
ing yourself."

Wendi gave Celine a sympathetic smile. "You
shouldn't feel guilty. Accidents happen."

"Guilt or anger is easier to feel than pain,"
Krystal added knowingly. "And anger can make
you do dumb things."

"Like call cheerleaders airheads when I don't
mean it." Celine wiped her eyes. "I'm so sorry for
taking my problems out on you guys. But I was
mad about staying with Gram and starting a new
school when I wanted to be near Mom. And I
blamed cheerleading for Mom's accident."

"Watching you cheer made your mother happy,"
Tabby pointed out. "And when she gets better,
it'll make her happy again."

"I hope so." Celine sighed. "I miss Mom so
much. And I was afraid that getting involved
with cheerleading would make me miss her
even more."

"Maybe cheering again will make you feel

closer to your mother," Tabby said gently. "And your grandmother is all for the idea. She wants you to be happy."

"Gram is great," Celine said, smiling for the first time. "She drives me to San Jose to visit Mom in the hospital twice a week. And Gram has been nagging me to make friends." Celine gave them a hopeful smile. "Guess I've finally taken her advice. I'd like to be your friend and part of your squad—if it's okay."

"It's more than okay. It's super!" Krystal exclaimed.

Anna flashed Celine a warm grin. "We're glad to have you with us."

"You bet!" Wendi reached across the table and shook Celine's hand. "Welcome to the Cheer Squad."

The new six-girl Cheer Squad met for practice the following night. Rachel was still on crutches, but she proved to be an enthusiastic audience. And Celine's gymnastic skills were awesome. She was so flexible that she could lie on her stomach and touch her feet to her head. And when she spun cartwheels, she was so graceful that it looked as if she were flying.

Still, there were problems. The biggest was choosing a cheer routine for the Harvest Festival. Anna and Tabby wanted to play it safe and do the "Go-Fight-Win" cheer. Krystal and Celine wanted to do a complicated performance cheer. Wendi thought there should be a way to combine both ideas, but she couldn't think of it. When no one could reach a decision, the girls turned to Aunt Carlotta for help.

"What should we do?" Wendy asked.

"I'm here to advise, not make your decisions for you," Aunt Carlotta said, resting one hand against the barre. "But I do have a suggestion."

Krystal raised her brows. "What?"

"I think it's time to vote on a squad captain. Then it will be *her* responsibility to choose the best routine."

"Great idea!" Krystal said enthusiastically— her tone making it clear she was the best one for the job.

Anna beamed at Krystal. "I nominate Krystal."

Tabby smiled at Wendi. "I nominate Wendi."

"Any other nominations?" Aunt Carlotta asked.

Wendi and her teammates shook their heads.

"Before we vote," Aunt Carlotta began, eyeing them with an amused smile, "I want to remind you of squad captain qualities: responsible, friendly, helpful, reliable, sensible, and someone who cares about her teammates."

Do I have all those qualities? Wendy wondered, crossing her fingers. Her heart pounded nervously. She wanted this so badly—but maybe Krystal wanted it, too. Who would win?

Krystal raised her hand.

"Yes?" Aunt Carlotta asked Krystal.

"I think our squad captain should have all those things you said," Krystal began, shifting her sitting position on the mat. "Someone who tries to help all her teammates—even when they don't appreciate it. And there's only one person who fits that description." Krystal's gaze drifted to Wendi. "I'm withdrawing my nomination in favor of Wendi."

"Me?" Wendi murmured in astonishment.

"You're perfect for squad captain," Krystal stated with a huge grin.

"Yay, Wendi!" Tabby hooted.

Wendi felt so happy, she barely heard the voting, which turned out to be unanimous. She was now officially the squad captain—a small but very special dream that had come true.

● ● ● ● ● ● ● ● ● ●

Seventeen

The new squad captain decided to blend an easy cheer with props for the Harvest Festival. When the others heard Wendi's idea for props, they applauded.

"Perfect. Right on target for our new squad," Tabby said with a grin.

"Cool idea," Celine approved. "Really creative."

"The audience will love it!" Krystal exclaimed.

"And I know just who to ask for the special props," Anna put in with enthusiasm.

Thursday night was their final practice before the talent show. Krystal breezed in fifteen minutes late because she'd been working on her retro singing act with Esteban. Her cheeks were flushed, and there was a twinkle in her eyes.

"It's about time," Anna said, giving her best friend a curious look. "I told you tonight was important. What kept you?"

"Romance! *Amor!* True love!" Krystal said, sitting cross-legged on the mat beside Anna. "Esteban told me he liked me a lot. Then he squeezed my hand. It was so, so, *so* super!"

The other Cheer Squad members giggled—except Anna, who simply rolled her eyes and groaned.

Aunt Carlotta shifted on her corner of the balance beam and offered Krystal a glowing smile. "Love is quite thrilling."

The squad got down to serious practicing then. Rachel sat on a stool with her crutches nearby. She couldn't jump or kick, but her arms were fine, so she would help with the props.

The routine is almost perfect, Wendi thought after they had practiced for two hours and were doing cooldown stretches. *Anna's cheers are stronger, Tabby's tumbling moves are smoother, Krystal isn't showing off quite as much, Celine is a quick learner, and I'm so busy being squad captain that most of the time I forget about my braces.* She glanced in the wall-length mirror and smiled widely. Silver teeth were still geeky—but actually kind of pretty. What had Tabby said? Like jewels.

Next time Darlene teases me, I think I'll just flash her my widest smile, Wendi decided mischievously. *That should confuse her big time.*

At the end of the practice session, Aunt Carlotta clapped. "Anna and I have a special surprise for you."

"What kind of surprise?" Wendi questioned.

"A terrific one especially for our new squad,"

Anna replied, reaching behind the desk and lifting up a plastic bag.

"You do the honors, Anna," Aunt Carlotta said.

Anna's black eyes sparkled as she held out the bag. "Here! Wendi, Tabby, Krystal, Rachel, and Celine—these are for you."

Wendi shared curious looks with her teammates. Then she stepped forward and eagerly peaked into the bag.

"I can't believe it!" Wendi exclaimed.

The other girls crowded around and also cried out with pleasure at the white T-shirts embossed with the logo CHEER SQUAD and matching green flared skirts.

"A skirt and T-shirt for each one of us," Anna said proudly. "Aunt Carlotta ordered the shirts, and I sewed the skirts."

"I knew you were a whiz with crafts, but these are awesome!" Krystal said, holding a shirt up to her chest so that the green-and-gold lettering showed up bold and bright.

Celine gazed at Anna with amazement. "You did this for *us?*"

"Aunt Carlotta and I did it together. The skirts were an easy pattern, just a few pieces to cut, stitch together, and hem. It was lots of fun—but hard to keep the secret. I almost told Krystal a dozen times."

"At last, the Cheer Squad will match," Wendi said happily. "No more crazy quilt outfits. And I love the colors!"

"I'm glad," Anna said, glowing with pleasure.

Wendi smiled to herself, and for the first time

all week she began to look forward to the Harvest Festival.

Watch out Darlene, Wendi thought confidently. *The Cheer Squad may be new, but we're here to stay.*

●●●●●●●●●●●

Eighteen

"Runaway pig!" a deep, gravelly voice boomed. "Come back here, Periwinkle!"

The Harvest Festival had just started, and Wendi and Tabby were standing underneath a shady elm tree waiting for the other members of the Cheer Squad to arrive. Hearing the excited shout, Wendi turned from Tabby to stare at a tall, gray-bearded man in denim overalls. The man waved his western hat in the air and ran across the grass—toward them.

From out of nowhere, a dog-size pinkish whirlwind squealed and brushed passed Wendi's white sneakers.

"*Eek!*" Wendi screamed, startled. "What was *that?*"

"A pig!" Tabby burst out.

"Periwinkle!" the bearded man yelled, almost knocking Wendi and Tabby over as he rushed by. "Git back here you good-for-nothin' bacon-bit bugger!"

Wendi watched the strange man chase the speeding pig around a Harvest Festival concession booth. Wendi shook her head and met Tabby's baffled gaze. "What's going on?"

"I'm not sure." Tabby giggled. "I guess they must be having pig races at this festival."

"But pig races means pigs race each other—not human against pig."

"I think the pig won," Tabby joked, which caused Wendi to double over with laughter.

"What's so funny?" Anna asked, joining them.

"You wouldn't believe us if we told you," Wendi said with a grin. Then she glanced around. "Where are Rachel, Celine, Krystal, and your aunt?"

"At the contest booth, finding out when our squad goes on."

"I hope we're not last," Tabby said anxiously. "I'm so nervous, I just want to get it over with."

"At least we won't be performing near mud puddles," Wendi said, picking up her tote bag that contained her Cheer Squad clothes and pompons.

"I've never been in a talent show before." Anna twisted her thick black ponytail and furrowed her brow. "A few dance recitals, but that was just for family. I'll be glad if I don't freeze and mess up the routine."

"You'll do fine," Wendi assured. "We all will." *I hope,* she added silently and crossed her fingers.

"Let's go to the contest booth and check out the schedule," Tabby suggested.

Wendi and Anna nodded; then the three hurried off.

As they passed a picnic area with scattered benches among oak, elm, and willow trees, Wendi suddenly stopped in her tracks.

"Oh!" she murmured, her hand flying to her mouth. With her other hand, she pointed to a group of girls positioned in two neat rows, waving glittery white pompons and moving with sharp uniform kicks that sent their shiny gold skirts swirling gracefully around their thighs.

"The Castle Hill Cheerleaders!" Tabby exclaimed. "They must be practicing."

"Shhsh!" Wendi clamped her hand over Tabby's mouth. "Keep it quiet, Miss Super Spy."

"We'd better go," Anna said worriedly.

"No. Let's watch." Wendi crouched with her friends behind a huge oak trunk. It would be embarrassing to be caught spying, but Wendi couldn't resist a peak at the competition.

Anna whispered, "Their outfits are so pretty. So professional. Better than anything I could sew."

"The skirts you made for us are wonderful," Tabby insisted. "But it *would* be nice to have matching poms like those. And get a look at their shoes. Megabucks."

"Their hair scrunchies sparkle," Wendi added wistfully, reaching up to touch the simple elastic-cotton scrunchie that held back her auburn hair. It was green to match her skirt. Okay, but dull compared to what the Castle Hill girls wore. No glitter. No glitz. No glamour.

Quietly, Wendi watched as Darlene spouted out directions and commands. No sign of Mr. Dittman, the squad coach. It appeared that Darlene was in charge.

"They're starting their routine from the top," Tabby said softly. "A hip-hop song. Nice beat. But they don't have any props."

"They don't need props," Wendi said enviously, noting that Darlene's hand motions had improved. LaShaun's timing still stank.

Apparently Darlene noticed LaShaun's timing, too, because she suddenly shouted, "Time out!" Then she strode over, wagged her finger at LaShaun, and began talking with angry gestures.

"I can't hear what she's saying," Tabby whispered. "But LaShaun looks ready to cry."

"Poor LaShaun," Anna said. "Darlene is really laying into her."

Wendi nodded, surprised at her sympathy for LaShaun. A squad captain should use gentle encouragement. Instead, Darlene seemed to prefer commando attack methods. Even worse, it looked like Darlene was cutting LaShaun from the squad. And a bewildered alternate, Autumn, was plopped into LaShaun's spot.

"I'm glad Darlene isn't *our* captain," Anna muttered.

"How can Darlene expect a flyer like Autumn to take over LaShaun's base position?" Wendi shook her head. "I can't stand to watch anymore. Let's go."

The Castle Hill Cheerleaders were forgotten

when the girls reached the contest booth and saw the contest schedule.

"Tenth place out of eleven acts!" Wendi exclaimed. "Almost last! And the Castle Hill Cheerleaders go on right before us. And can you believe who follows us: Logie Foster and his dancing pigs!"

"It's my fault our squad has the tenth spot," Krystal admitted. She wore a braided headband over her straight, long blond hair, multicolored strands of beads, and a flowing lavender skirt. "I told the contest officials that I needed time to change outfits. Esteban and I go on first. I can't wait!"

Wendi gazed with wonder at Krystal. *How can she be so excited? I'm so nervous, my hands are shaking. I keep imagining all the things that could go wrong. I could drop my pompons or the props. My mind might go blank and I'll forget all the steps. Or a sudden storm might form, and I'll be struck by lightning, and my braces will glow like silver neon beacons.*

"Nervous?" Celine asked, giving Wendi a probing look.

Wendi smiled. "No . . . well, maybe a little."

"I'm a jumble of nerves," Celine confided. "I haven't cheered in front of an audience since Mom's accident. I keep thinking of her and wishing she were here."

Wendi just nodded, since she couldn't come up with anything comforting to say. She'd hate to have her mother—or any family member—in the hospital. She knew she was lucky to have a healthy, supportive family. Her parents and Valerie had already found front row seats in the talent show audience.

Esteban came over carrying a guitar and looking as retro-sixties as Krystal. He also looked uneasy, but when his gaze fell on Krystal, he brightened.

True love, Wendi thought. *Someday a boy will look at me like that. Maybe in eighth grade.*

"I'm on!" Krystal announced, jumping with excitement. "Come on Esteban. Our adoring public awaits!"

Esteban turned a pea-colored shade of green and numbly followed Krystal.

The Harvest Festival Talent Show was beginning!

Once on the stage, Esteban's color returned, and he strummed his guitar like he'd been born with it in his arms. And Krystal was fabulous! Her voice was smooth and tangy, with a haunting quality. She danced and sang her heart out.

Wendi applauded so hard, her palms ached— and her pride in her friends soared to the stars.

The Cheer Squad didn't get a chance to watch the next several acts because they had to change into their outfits, fix their hair, and put on makeup. Wendi thought they looked great in white, green, and gold. But they didn't have the polished appearance of the Castle Hill Cheerleaders. And, sadly, all Cheer Squad members had different colored poms.

But our props will spice up our act, Wendi thought hopefully. Then she and her teammates left the rest room/dressing room. As they stepped outside, Wendi heard the next act being announced via microphone: the Castle Hill Cheerleaders.

Our competition, Wendi thought nervously. *The war lines are drawn, and now the battle begins.*

●●●●●●●●●●●

Nineteen

Wendi held on tightly to her pompons as she watched the Castle Hill girls take their places and drop to a one-knee position with their arms straight down, their poms brushing the stage. The tall blond man who was introducing the Castle Hill Cheerleaders wore a shirt logo advertising himself as the King of Plumbing. Wendi guessed he was Darlene's father—or "the Toilet King," as Tabby once joked.

"They look good," Tabby whispered, standing beside Wendi off stage, not far from where the rest of the Cheer Squad stood talking in an excited group.

"So will we," Wendi replied. *Just not as good,* she thought enviously. *As the squad captain, I'll have to come up with some fund-raiser ideas so we can get matching green or gold pompons.*

Tabby pointed toward the audience. "There's your sister."

Wendi's gaze shifted, and she felt a wave of happiness. Yes, it was Valerie sitting with her parents. Beside them, an older woman with gray-flecked ebony hair looked familiar. Memory clicked, and Wendi recognized Celine's grandmother. There was a proud expression on the older woman's face.

Celine may not have her mother, but I'm glad she has such a supportive grandmother, Wendi thought with a smile. *And maybe the next time the Cheer Squad performs, Celine's mother will be out of the hospital and in the audience, too.*

Wendi noticed that Tabby was still studying the audience, as if searching for someone.

"Is your mom here?" Wendi questioned.

"Yeah. Fifth row. Adam, too—which is a pleasant shock. But I had hoped . . ." Tabby bit her lip and shrugged. "It was dumb to hope for anything. I should know better by now."

"Your father?" Wendi asked gently.

Tabby nodded. "When I told him about the talent show, he said he'd try to make it. Something must have come up. Like always." Tabby's expression changed swiftly. "The Castle Hill Cheerleaders are starting!"

"And when they're done, we're next," Wendi said, her fingers clasped tightly around her pompons.

There were twelve girls on the Castle Hill squad, and they began in two lines of six; kicking, waving their poms, and chanting a rousing cheer for the football Knights.

It was a smooth, upbeat routine—heavy on

cheer moves and light on gymnastics. Most of the eighth grade cheerleaders were skilled in gymnastics, but only a few of the seventh grade girls were—and some of these girls (all popular friends of Darlene's) moved like stiff, unoiled robots. One girl in particular was painfully awkward.

Wendi gazed sympathetically at Autumn. It was obvious she didn't know the moves very well. Her smile looked strained as she struggled to keep up with the others. The girl next to Autumn cartwheeled across the stage, and Autumn jumped into a cartwheel, too. Unfortunately, she was a beat behind.

Her feet sailed like windmills in the air just as Darlene catapulted backward with a back flip—and *crash!* Autumn's white sneaker struck Darlene on the leg. Both girls cried out as they stumbled and fell down in a tangled heap.

Instead of recovering quickly and resuming the routine, Darlene started yelling at Autumn. Wendi's mouth dropped in astonishment as Darlene's angry words drifted to her—"Idiot! Moron! Klutz!"—and the insults raged on until Darlene's father had to take his daughter by the arm and pull her off the stage.

The audience buzzed with whispers and exclamations. Before Wendi and her teammates had a chance to say anything, a distraught talent show official rushed over and told them to hurry and get on stage.

Aunt Carlotta clapped her hands and ordered, "Girls! Take your positions! The Cheer Squad is *on!*"

Wendi exchanged a terrified, anxious, excited glance with Tabby. This was it! A strange calmness filled Wendi, and she suddenly felt like she could achieve anything she strived for. She knew the routine backward, forward, and sideways. And unlike Darlene, she wasn't going to use her squad captain title as a weapon to push others around. She trusted her teammates to do their best. And she would also do *hers*.

Aunt Carlotta helped Rachel hobble on her crutches to a chair in a strategic position on the stage. She carried two very important props in her arms, and at a prearranged cue, she would be ready for her part of the routine.

And then music rang out—a fun, bouncy rock beat that swelled like a wave of energy in Wendi's soul. The Cheer Squad danced onto the stage, and then the music faded away as they began to chant:

> *The basketball Knights*
> *Are on the ball.*
> *They're the team to beat,*
> *The best of all.*
> *Dribble, pass, and throw,*
> *They always shoot to win.*
> *So go mighty Knights,*
> *Let the game begin!*

At this point, the Cheer Squad dropped their poms. While Tabby, Celine, and Krystal continued to clap and chant for the Knights, Wendi, and Anna did a body roll to the floor, came up with a synchronized toe touch, then did a double pirouette over to Rachel.

Wendi reached for one of the bright-orange props in Rachel's arms: a basketball. And Anna grabbed the other prop: a slender netted basketball hoop.

Anna did some funky moves with her feet and held the hoop straight out. Wendi gracefully tossed the ball through the net, then retrieved and passed the ball to Tabby. Wendi cartwheeled over to join a line with Tabby, Krystal, and Celine.

They chanted as baskets were made:

> *Shoot for a basket,*
> *Knights to win!*
> *B-A-S-K-E-T,*
> *Basket!*

When they said the final "basket," it was Tabby's turn to throw the ball into Anna's net. Hoop shot! The audience applauded like crazy.

The Cheer Squad continued to chant as Krystal caught the ball before it bounced twice. It was Krystal's turn to sink the ball. Then Celine's. And they ended the prop routine with Anna handing the net off to Rachel and slam-dunking the ball one last time. The routine finished with poms high as the Cheer Squad cartwheeled into synchronized splits.

Wendi's heart pounded wildly, excitedly, and she flashed a finale smile at the audience. She'd never felt so jazzed in her life—and it was fantastic. Being a cheerleader was everything she dreamed . . . even better!

And the applause continued to sing in her head as the Cheer Squad left the stage. She dimly heard someone announce Logie Foster and his dancing pigs, but she was too busy jumping and sharing high fives with her teammates.

Wendi knew they'd done well—they were a success. And that mattered more than beating Darlene or taking home a first place award. It didn't matter who actually won. In her heart, Wendi already felt like a winner. Still, it was exciting when a newspaper photographer snapped their picture for the *Kalaroosa Kapers*.

But excitement changed to jitters a short time later when a contest official stood up on stage and prepared to announce the Harvest Festival talent contest results.

Twenty

The chubby red-haired man held the mike to his mouth and cleared his throat. Wendi squeezed Tabby's hand and stared anxiously ahead.

"We'll begin with fifth place," the official declared. He checked a paper and announced, "Congratulations to our fifth place winners: the Castle Hill Cheerleaders!"

Applause rang out. The official looked around, waiting for someone from the Castle Hill Cheerleaders to appear. The applause dwindled to silence, but there was no sign of any Castle Hill girls.

"I can't believe they ditched the contest!" Wendi whispered to Tabby.

"That's terrible sportsmanship," Tabby hissed back. "They probably only got an award because everyone feels sorry for them!"

Finally after a few awkward moments, the red-haired man went to fourth place. "Logie Foster and his dancing pigs!" More applause. Tall, bearded Logie strutted on stage with three pigs on leashes. Wendi couldn't tell which one was Periwinkle.

Third place went to a tap dancing brother and sister act.

Wendi crossed her fingers, realizing only two spots were left. Several singers had been really good—especially Krystal. And Wendi thought uneasily, *I'll just die if the Cheer Squad doesn't place at all!*

But she was saved from an early, tragic death by disappointment. The Cheer Squad made second place. The award was a gift certificate for free pizzas at a nearby pizza parlor.

And then first place was announced—and Krystal squealed louder than any of Logie Foster's pigs when her name and Esteban's were called. She was so excited that she did a cartwheel as she sprinted to the stage with Esteban. They won a trophy and a hundred dollars to share.

When the excitement died down and people started to leave the contest area, Wendi turned to her teammates and adviser.

"As squad captain, I have an important suggestion to make," Wendi said in a teasing voice.

"Suggest away," Aunt Carlotta said with a wave of her hand.

"How important?" Celine asked.

"Oh . . . *very.* I think we should celebrate our success in a fitting manner." Wendi flashed a mischievous grin and held up a long white envelope with the words SECOND PLACE PRIZE printed on it. "Let's go out for pizza! All in favor say aye!"

Everyone voted enthusiastically. There wasn't a single nay to be heard.

That night, Wendi wrote in her computer diary:

Today the Cheer Squad won its first award—and it was delicious! We ate pizza with our friends and family and had a wonderful time. Of course, performing on the stage was the most wonderful part of today. I loved dancing, cheering, and hearing applause. Now I know how Valerie felt all those years as a cheerleader: special.

•••••••••••

Épilogue

A few days later, Wendi knelt on her bedroom carpet and reached underneath her bed. Her fingers touched something hard, rectangular, and thin. She withdrew the scrapbook and placed it gently on her bedspread.

"The Cheer Squad's official scrapbook," she murmured.

Then she walked over to her desk, picked up an article cut from the newspaper, and some glue.

She reread the newspaper article's headline: A CHEER FOR SECOND PLACE. It was a brief piece that only ran for one column, but it listed all the Cheer Squad names—singling out Wendi Holcroft as squad captain. And it was the first clipping to go in the scrapbook.

The first of many more to come, Wendi knew in her heart. *And someday the win will be as big as they get,* Wendi mused. *The Cheer Squad will compete in the nationals and win big time. I don't know when, but I know it will happen. And I can't wait. . . .*

If you enjoyed *Cheer Squad #1: Crazy for Cartwheels,*
sample the following brief selection from

CHEER SQUAD #2: SPIRIT SONG

from Avon Camelot.

Go green!
Go gold!
The Castle Hill Knights
Are strong and bold!
Go gold!
Go green!
The Knights will be
The winning te—

"Anna! You're facing the wrong way!"

Anna Herrera stopped instantly, her ponytail flipping forward and slapping her cheek. Startled, she looked at the Cheer Squad's captain, Wendi Holcroft. "Sorry, Wendi."

"Hey, we all make mistakes." Wendi swiped her perspiring forehead with her hand and grinned. "Just remember to spin in place on the word 'winning.' Then you and Tabby will back flip into the splits while the rest of us lift our pompons high in a *V*."

"I got it." Anna managed to return Wendi's grin. Anna always tried hard to be cheerful, no matter how embarrassed or upset she might feel. And right now she felt *really* embarrassed. She hated messing up her squad's practice—especially today, when Coach Kendall was due to show up any moment.

"So let's take it from the top!" Wendi called out, and the six girls split into two lines and resumed practice.

Anna tried hard to concentrate. As she sang out "Go gold, go green!" with enthusiasm, she counted out the beats in her head: *One, two, side step, three four, spin* . . . And at the end of the routine, she remembered to spin around and flip backward in synch with Tabby. Success!

Relieved, Anna let out a shaky breath as she stood up.

"Great, everyone!" Wendi called out, dropping her poms on the wooden floor. "Let's take a five-minute break. Afterward, we'll work on sideline chants."

"Maybe by then Coach Kendall will have shown up," Krystal Carvell said as she trailed behind Anna. "Why isn't he here?"

"I've been wondering the same thing," Anna admitted, sipping water out of a plastic bottle. The Cheer Squad usually practiced at Anna's Aunt Carlotta's Victorian mansion, but Coach

Kendall had asked the girls to practice in the gym after school today. No reason was given at all. Weird.

"Coach Kendall has never been very interested in our squad. Why now?" Krystal asked, her blue eyes wide with curiosity.

"Basketball season begins in a few weeks." Anna sank into a metal chair, stretching out her legs to ease her aching muscles. "Maybe he wants to check out our routines."

"Then he should be here watching." Krystal pushed away wild strands of honey-blond hair that escaped from her ponytail. "I thought we were going to have an audience, so I spent hours choosing just the right outfit. And for *nothing!*"

Anna couldn't resist a grin. Krystal always looked dazzling—even when she wasn't trying. The other girls wore comfy T-shirts and shorts to practice, but not Krystal. Shimmery black leggings molded to her long shapely legs; an embroidered denim vest fit over a silky silver blouse; and her thick blond hair was pulled back with a glittery silver scrunchie.

"Coach Kendall will show up soon," Anna said optimistically.

"Maybe." Krystal's tone was skeptical. "But he only organized our squad to inspire spirit in his basketball players. He's never acted like *our* coach. Thank goodness your aunt stepped in as the adult in charge of our squad—or there never would have been a Cheer Squad."

Anna flashed a proud smile. "Aunt Carlotta loves being our adviser."

"Your aunt is terrific," Krystal agreed. "She helps without being bossy. With her as an adviser, we don't need a coach."

"What are you two whispering about?" someone asked.

Anna looked up as auburn-haired Wendi Holcroft joined them. A few weeks ago, Wendi had been voted in as squad captain, and she was terrific at the job. She had lots of spirit, she came up with creative routines on her computer, and she'd even started a Cheer Squad scrapbook.

"We were just talking about Coach Kendall," Anna told Wendi. "If he isn't going to watch us cheer, why did he arrange this practice?"

"I wish I knew." Wendi's hazel eyes grew serious. "I hope he doesn't have bad news for us—like maybe the basketball players don't want cheerleaders after all. I'll just die if he cancels the Cheer Squad."

"That won't happen," Anna assured quickly. She had no idea if her words were true. She just couldn't stand to see one of her friends upset. "Our squad did terrific at the Harvest Festival talent show. Coach Kendall *has* to be impressed."

"I think we'll find out soon," Krystal said ominously. She pointed to the front of the gym.

The short, athletic-looking basketball coach had arrived.

Anna clutched the sides of the metal chair,

growing tense as she watched Wendi hurry over to Coach Kendall.

"What's he saying to her?" Krystal whispered anxiously.

"I can't read lips," Anna whispered back. "But Wendi looks uptight. And Coach Kendall is heading for the stage."

Anna's heart pounded. What if Wendi was right about Coach Kendall wanting to cancel the Cheer Squad? But that couldn't happen! Not after all their hard work!

In a month, the Cheer Squad had come a long way. They'd survived rumors of being the loser squad, and they'd grown from a four-girl squad to six. They'd even won second place at a talent show. And they were getting better every day.

The Cheer Squad can't be canceled! Anna thought anxiously. *It wouldn't be fair!*

Coach Kendall now stood on the stage. "Listen up, gals," he called out loudly. "I have an important announcement."

Anna reached out and squeezed Krystal's hand for support.

"First of all, I want to congratulate you. I was happy to hear you did so well in the talent show. Made me real proud."

Anna let out a shaky breath. So far, so good.

"But as I told you before, I don't know much about cheering." Coach Kendall ran his fingers over his smooth buzz-cut. "And I've felt bad I haven't been able to help you gals out. So I'm not going to be your coach anymore—"

Anna shot Krystal a terrified look.

"—because our school has hired a new gym teacher with college cheerleading experience," Coach Kendall continued with a grin. "Her name is Miss Laing, and starting Monday, she's going to coach the Cheer Squad!"

Read All the Stories by
Beverly Cleary